全民英檢篇
English
續·偽英語教科書

Bob is pinching his nipple to signify his disagreement.

前言

本書不是以報考TOEIC、英語能力檢定考試的考生為對象，而是將Twitter上面發表「多讀無益 TOEIC英文單字」的內容出版成《偽英語教科書》系列書籍，這次是《續‧偽英語教科書》。不好意思這系列叢書出版得落落長，讓各位見笑了。

在廣大浩瀚的英文學習書中，您一時「福至心靈」拿起了本書，在此深深作揖拜謝。但在此還是要先向您確認一下，本書書名是《偽英語教科書》，不是《真英語教科書》，請讀者慎重確認，千萬不要搞錯了。書名取得讓人看了一頭霧水，增添各位的不少麻煩；本書是完全背道而馳的教學內容，千萬不要搞錯以為是《速讀英文單字》、《高分目標1900》、《DUO 3.0》等書。雖然書名完全風馬牛不相及，但有的讀者還是會看錯，想必一定是平日非常勞心勞力所致；如果看錯成是《DUO 3.0》那歹誌就大條了，請趕快回家休息。

此外，或許有人會把「考試不考」這句話擴大解讀成「在日常生活中可以使用」；但很抱歉，因為又是您想太多了。本書中的單字、例句不僅在考試中用不到，在商務上、學校裡和日常生活中也都派不上用場，全部內容都是如地雷般的燙手山芋。或許又有人會把「考試不會出現」這部分誤解成「泡妞必勝」的意思，但再度向您說聲抱歉，這也許是您精蟲衝腦所致。本書中出現的單字、例句，不僅在聯誼中不適用，在相親、上酒家、約會時都極度不合用。

再者，或許有人會以為既然叫做「實踐篇」，肯定能派上什麼用場吧？抱持這最後一絲希望的讀者又要跟您說抱歉了。在前作與本書中所介紹的「考試不會出現的非重要單字」，是為了讓讀者能深刻記住這件事，所以透過各種手段來「實踐」它，並不是說本書內容可以派上用場去實踐它的意思。

如果上述的事項都無法說動您、把命豁出去說什麼都要看《續‧偽英語教科書》，在此向這些大無畏的讀者深表謝意。最後，敝人再多嘴詢問一下：「購買本書的您是不是腦袋被K到了？還是快去檢查一下為佳啊！」

吾等日本人儘管在學校教育中長期學習英語，還是無法隨心所欲使用英語。在社會環境日益國際化的今天，英語成為無可取代的全球共通語言。再者，隨著科技演進，除了透過會話進行溝通，現在還可透過海外網頁的瀏覽、電郵、推特和臉書來進行線上的溝通，隨處都可使用到英語。世界與您的距離正在逐漸縮短，也許有一天您會突然身陷在非得使用英語不可的情況中也不一定。對於遭遇這樣困境的人而言，能夠有一本在最短時間最有效學會英語的參考書，正是他們最求之不得的。

本書深切了解讀者的熱烈渴望，由於任重道遠，於是拱手將這任務承讓給其它的參考書，反其道而行希望作出一本花費最長學習時間的參考書。為何要背道而馳呢？在浩瀚的知識深淵中，即使身為作者的我也無從得知。不過正如孫子兵法書中所說「迂廻之計」，為了達成目的不走最短的距離反繞道而行，說不定能更快達到目的。雖然曲解原意，卻不失為真理。據說英語單字數量有幾百萬個之多，要考到TOEIC 900分以上需要具備15000個單字程度，像本系列書籍《偽英語教科書》所介紹的單字只有150個，以這數量來計算的話一輩子要學完幾乎是不可能的事情。不過，可能性愈低才愈足以激發鬥志，這正是把《賭博默示錄》奉為聖經，身為上班族我們的成長心聲啊！

最後，繼前作之後，居然心胸廣大願意接受「考試不會出現」這種不事生產的想法，並且將它出版成書的編輯品川先生；還有將想法很酷獸的本書設計成漂亮書籍的木庭先生；以及絞盡腦汁將不可理喻的文章畫成有趣插畫的千葉小姐。特地遠道從英國前來，認真校對愚不可及的英文，並且擔任配音的山繆先生，還有椿先生、齊藤小姐，在此真心向你們致謝。另外，每天在網路上為我的狗屁英文按讚的粉絲們，真的非常感謝你們，請接受我的一拜。

使用本書時的注意事項

第一段　考試不會出現的英文單字

千里之途始於起步。首先透過短文來充分理解什麼叫做考試不會出現的核心觀念吧！

第二段　考試不會出現的英文會話

用兵貴在神速。熟悉短文之後，一口氣將會話文累加上去。將學習到的會話利用在日常生活之中也是非常重要的。

第三段　考試不會出現的長文解讀

先大量後優質。利用長文章充分領教英文的威力。在文法脈絡中，即使平常用不到的單字也能因此有效的記住實際用法。

第四段　考試不會出現的看圖說故事

每張圖會標出4則短文。選出最能「適切符合」圖中的狀況和登場人物心理的其中一則敘述，並且要裝出自己很用功的樣子。只要裝得非常用功就更能顯現出拚命三郎的模樣。

第五段　考試不會出現的文法問題

耳朵的裡面有耳洞。耳洞很容易漏聽，所以不能拚命死記，而是要像灌漿進去讓身體產生自然反應。一直反覆練習容易出錯的地方，直到可以熟稔記住考試不考的每個單字至止。

將第一段～第五段牢牢記在腦海裡，您就站在不輸人的考前出發起跑點上了。只是一起跑就會落後十萬八千里，這部分還是要請您多利用一般的參考書好好用功吧！

目錄

關於英式英語

本書使用的英語都是「英式英語」。完全不使用在日本的英語教育中普遍使用的美式英語，
就是要將考試不會出現的理念從頭到尾發揮到最徹底。

CHAPTER 1

考試不會出現的英文單字

50 NONESSENTIAL VOCABULARY

徹底分析入學考與各種資格考，嚴選50個非重要英語單字＋50條例句，但考上與否將不會由此決定。建議各位反覆練習直到生根腦海中，讓我們邁向考試合格最長的距離吧！

001

google

［谷哥(搜尋)］

例句

「為什麼不三『谷哥』茅廬呢？」
諸葛亮對劉備愛理不理的回答。

"Why not google it?"
Zhuge Liang said to Liu Bei dryly.

☞ 既生「谷哥」何生亮？

002

cockroach

［小強］

例句

這隻小強年紀雖小，卻很穩重。

The cockroach is very mature for his age.

☞ 應該只是吃了蟑腦丸，其實已經神智不清了吧？

003

caustic lime

［ 生石灰 ］

例句

**群馬縣得天獨厚擁有廣大的土地和生石灰，
最適合做棒球打者準備區。**

With its vast land area and bountiful reserves of caustic lime,
the Gunma prefecture is as perfect as an on-deck circle.

☞ 可以與蔥、蒟蒻並列為群馬縣的三大主要產業。

004

gay

［男同志］

例句

鮑伯的房子每當有重口味男同志經過時，就會搖晃個不停。

Bob's house shakes
every time a hard-core gay man passes.

☞ 注意：搖晃的是鮑伯的房子，並不是鮑伯的屁股。

005

bamboo spear

［竹槍］

例句

群馬縣為了嚇止武力，儲備了大量的竹槍。

Gunma prefecture possesses a massive number of bamboo spears as a deterrent.

☞ 群馬縣民認為用竹槍就足夠抵抗核武了。

006

flat-chested

［貧乳的］

例句

「哎呀，妳看起來一臉貧乳的樣子，
快回家去好好休息吧！」

"Oh, you look flat-chested.
I think you should have a good rest."

☞ 與貧血一樣，休息就能恢復嗎？

007

magic circle

［魔法陣］

例句

「嘿，這魔法陣裡有一根頭髮！」

"Hey! There's a hair
in this magic circle."

☞ 看起來好像是那個「什麼」毛…

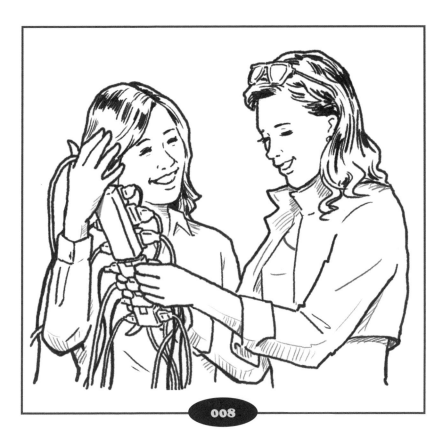

008

octopus wiring

［延長線］

例句

「好好看的延長線喔！」
「謝謝，我請專家特別設計的。」

"Fantastic octopus wiring!"
"Thanks, I had a pro do it."

☞ 請的是哪種專家啊？肯定不是電器專家。

009

summon

［召喚］

例句

「經理，不好意思打擾您召喚龍，
有找您的電話。」

"Boss, I'm sorry to interrupt your summoning spell,
but there is a call for you."

☞ 討厭，頭才剛冒出來的說！

010

change-up

[變化球]

例句

「克拉拉大小姐
居然投出了變化球！」

"Clara is...
Clara is throwing a change-up!"

☞ 不僅能站起來，還能投出變化球，
這就是阿爾卑斯山的神奇治癒力！

011

marlin

［馬林魚］

例句

「要我用肛門壓制住馬林魚，辦不到！」
「嘴上無毛的，閃邊！」

"There's no way I can push a marlin into my anus!"
"Hey, kid. Back off!"

☞ 肛是老的辣。你看，這不就肛肛好嗎？

012

crab louse

［陰蝨］

例句

我是你從陷阱中救出來的陰蝨。

I am the crab louse you saved
from the trap.

☞ 蟲子雖小，五臟俱全。陰蝨報恩，一生寄生。

013

pond snail

［田螺］

例句

鄰居不小心，
開車壓到了我的田螺。

Our neighbor carelessly drove
over my pond snail.

☞ 到底眼睛是看哪裡？田螺長那麼大，開車居然也能壓到！

014

spring bonito

［初鰹魚］

例句

從這個角度看，
部門經理簡直就像一隻初鰹魚。

From this angle,
our department manager looks like a spring bonito.

☞ 小心不要被抓去做生魚片了。

015

Excalibur

[王者之劍]

例句

因為沒有馬桶座墊，
勇者只好拿出王者之劍來代替。

As the toilet seat was missing,
the Hero hesitantly substituted it with Excalibur.

☞ 幸好不是拿劍來擦屁股……

016

goomba

[磨菇]

例句

瑪利歐兄弟的鞋底下
肯定有不少磨菇的肉片。

If you take a look at the sole of Mario's shoe,
you will find it covered in goomba meat.

☞ 唔哇，要替牠們報仇！

017

reindeer

［馴鹿］

例句

「呵呵呵，聖誕老頭，
不要小看我們馴鹿的力量！」

"Hehehe Santa Claus.
You should never underestimate the power of a reindeer."

☞ 能載著聖誕老人在世界各地奔跑，想必不會是弱者。

018

get down on all fours

［橫躺］

例句

「就從昨天停下來的地方重新開始。
請脫光衣服，全裸橫躺！」

"Let's start from where we left off yesterday.
Please take your clothes off and get down on all fours."

☞ 不知道想要幹什麼，但就不能換個麻豆嗎？

019

wooden gong

［木魚］

例句

「係金ㄟ？
這個價錢就能買到木魚和增量的胸罩？」

"Really?
This price includes a wooden gong and a volume up bra?"

☞ 很特別的異業組合，是要賣給貧乳的尼姑嗎？

Thwack

［重擊咒語］

例句

「呃，什麼？我聽不到！請你再說大聲一點！」
「札拉基！」「呀啊啊啊！」

"What? I can't hear you. Can you speak up?"
"Thwack." "Arghhh!"

☞ 到底是重聽還是咒語奏效，究竟是哪一個啊？

021

best-before date

[賞味期限]

例句

「抱歉，妳的賞味期限已經過了。」

"I'm afraid to say this,
but you are passed your best-before date."

☞ 沒關係，不是保存期限就好了。

022

acorn

［板栗］

例句

精密檢查的結果顯示，不是腫瘤，只是板栗。

A detailed examination revealed that it wasn't cancer,
just an acorn.

☞ 精密檢查結果「栗栗」在目。
在檢查前應該就能避免這種情況了吧？

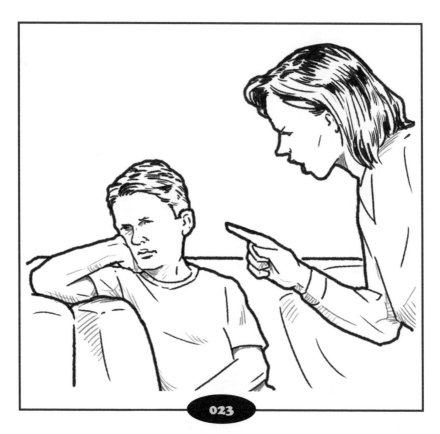

023

bowel

［腸子］

例句

「你的腸子跑出來了，
把它收進去！」

"Your bowel is out. Tuck it in."

☞ 正妹不喜歡疝氣迴腸的男生喔！

024

taro

［芋頭］

例句

這間學校包括芋頭在內，
總共有26位老師。

There are 26 teachers,
including one taro, in this school.

☞ 芋仔蕃薯都有算進去。

025

river crab

［河蟹］

例句

「時間到！每個人把手上的河蟹放下來。」

"Time's up! Put down your river crabs."

☞ 從最後一排開始一隻一隻疊上來交到蟹老闆手上。

026

cleavage

［事業線］

例句

史蒂芬妮的事業線
在道德上是不正確的。

Stefanie's cleavage is morally bankrupt.

☞ 換個時間地點可能就大大的正確。

027

crop circle

［麥田圈］

例句

公司的CEO在離婚之後，
每天都在田裡做麥田圈。

Our CEO has been making crop circles every day
since he got divorced.

☞ 看來要回到正軌，可能還需要等做一個巨石陣出來以後。

028

designated hitter

［指定打者］

例句

「乘客中，有沒有人是指定打者？」

"Is there a designated hitter
in the house?"

☞ 到底是落後多少分？

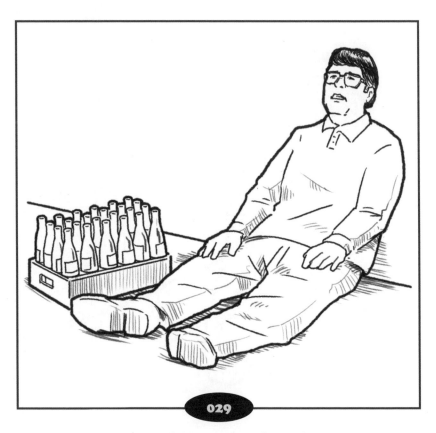

029

Molotov cocktail

[莫洛托夫汽油瓶]

例句

因為被贈品吸引，
結果買了一打莫洛托夫汽油瓶。

Tempted by the free gift,
I bought a dozen Molotov cocktail bottles.

☞ 贈品是馬卡茸嗎？

030

miniskirt

［迷你裙］

例句

總經理差一點窒息死掉，
因為他吞下迷你裙卡住喉嚨。

The general manager almost died
from choking on a miniskirt.

☞ 沒有標示「不能吞食」，打官司說不定有勝算。

031

virginity

［童貞］

例句

「可惡，那婆娘偷走了最寶貴的東西，你的童貞！」

"No, she stole something quite precious.
Your virginity."

☞ 快去要回來呀！

RITZ

［ 麗滋餅乾 ］

例句

靖子為了証明麗滋餅乾派對的存在
而奉獻了一輩子的歲月。

Yasuko dedicated her life
to proving the existence of RITZ Parties.

☞ 遺憾的是迄今還是無法証明是否存在。

033

basic skin-care product

［基礎化妝品］

例句

士兵們丟下基礎化妝品投降了。

The soldiers threw down their basic skin-care products
and surrendered.

☞ 既然不能夠保養肌膚，繼續作戰下去也就沒有意義了。

034

Gunma Prefecture

［群馬縣］

例句

這個實驗是要証明群馬縣是否真實存在。

This experiment is designed to determine
the existence of Gunma Prefecture.

☞ 如果真的存在就好了⋯⋯

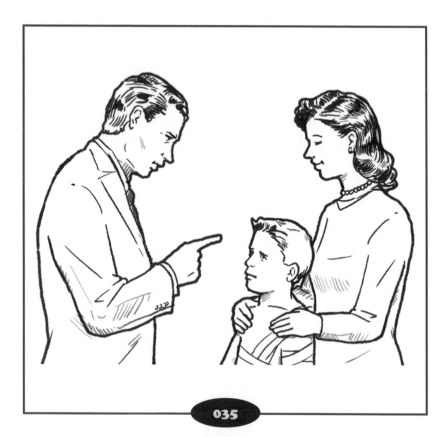

035

machine gun

［機關槍］

例句

「不要因為被機關槍掃到手臂和肚子，
就哭哭啼啼的！」

"Don't whine just because someone shot you
in the arm and stomach with a machine gun."

☞ 正妹喜歡機關槍，不喜歡娘娘腔！

036

honey trap

［美人計］

例句

「別慌張，
這是孔明的美人計啦！」

"Don't panic.
This is Zhuge Liang's honey trap."

☞ 魏國大臣司馬懿該糟了！

037

paw pad

［肉球］

例句

「為了見証我倆的友情，
把俺的肉球收下吧！」

"Please accept these paw pads
as a token of friendship."

☞ 哇，人家一直都很想要的說。

038

murder case

［謀殺案件］

例句

「抱歉我遲到了，
剛才被捲入謀殺案件。」

"Sorry, I'm late.
I was caught in a murder case."

☞ 說抱歉就能了事了嗎？

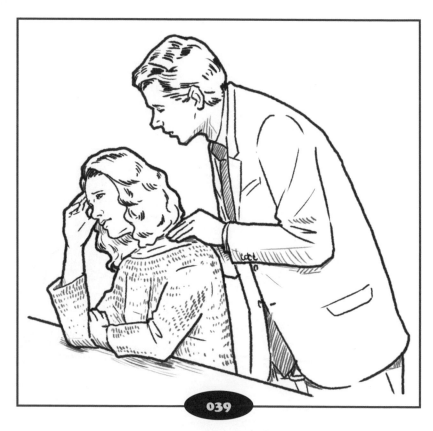

039

night raid

［夜襲］

例句

「史蒂芬妮，妳的鎖鏈盔甲的線頭裂開了。」
「不玩了，今晚本來要夜襲的說！」

"Stefanie, you've got a run in your chain mail."
"Oh my, I'm supposed to have a night raid tonight!"

☞ 敢問是菊花夜襲軍嗎？

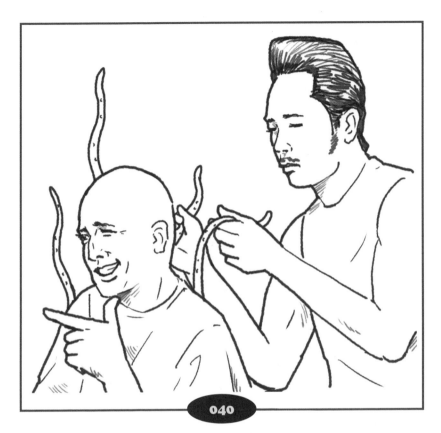

040

tentacle

［觸手］

例句

「客人你的觸手簡直就像新鮮的義大利麵！」

"Your tentacles look just like fresh pasta."

☞ 應該不是正妹的菜吧？

041

biological weapon
［生化武器］

例句

孫女買給我的生化武器真是幫了大忙。

"The biological weapons that my granddaughter bought for me, were very helpful."

☞ 阿嬤，妳殺人如麻了！

042

Buddhist sutra

［佛經］

例句

和尚應觀眾的熱烈要求再度登台，
念了自己創作的佛經。

The monk came back to the stage for an encore
and chanted his original Buddhist sutra.

☞ 早念早超生。

043

tea stalk

［茶梗］

例句

「抱歉打擾您的興致，
那不是茶梗，是陰毛。」

"I hate to disappoint you,
but this isn't a tea stalk. It's a pubic hair."

☞ 呸呸呸，真是不吉利。

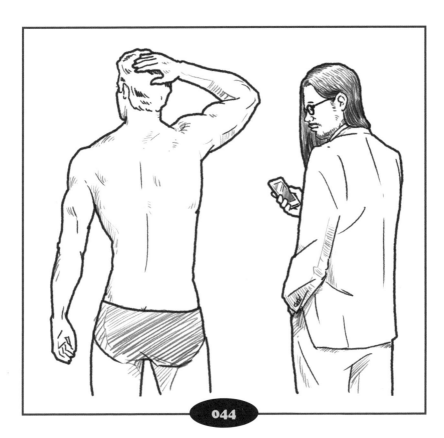

044

anal sphincter

［肛門括約肌］

例句

「你的肛門括約肌好像無法迎合我的需求。」

"Your anal sphincter doesn't quite appeal to me."

☞ 是不是搞錯部位了啊？

045

sex change operation

［變性手術］

例句

尼克剛工作時的情緒很低落，
不過去做了變性手術，立馬就找回元氣。

**Business matters took their toll on Nick,
but he soon recovered and had a sex change operation.**

☞ 也找回太多了吧！

046

hemostasis

[止血]

例句

「今天天氣真好，要不要來止血呢？」

"It's such a nice day!
How about some hemostasis?"

☞ 即使天氣不佳，也希望能替他止血！

047

Muay Thai kick

［ 泰拳踢 ］

例句

泰拳踢是日本人在處罰別人時
最重要的手段之一。

A Muay Thai kick is one of the most important methods
for Japanese people to punish someone.

☞ 對於動不動就被叫出來踢的泰國人也算是一種處罰。

048

stun gun

［電擊棒］

例句

「孩子的媽，有沒有看到我的電擊棒？」
「討厭，你這死鬼……」

"Honey, do you know where my stun gun is?"
"Oh, no, dear..."

☞ 這對尪某是在放什麼閃啦？

049

telekinesis

［念力］

例句

史蒂芬妮用念力來調整鮑伯雞雞的位置。

Stefanie adjusted Bob's penis position by telekinesis.

☞ 有這特異功能好歹去當個神盾局特工吧！

050

gel-like

［膠滴滴的］

例句

「這真的是傳說中的盾牌嗎？
已經都變得膠滴滴的……」

"Hey, is this really the legendary shield?
It's gel-like..."

☞ 肯定是保存方法出了問題！

經理的召喚術
Manager's Summoning

"I'm sorry to interrupt you when you're summoning a dragon, but there is a call for you."

「經理，抱歉打擾您召喚龍，有找您的電話。」

"I'm sorry to interrupt you when you're summoning an accident faker, but there is a call for you."

「經理，抱歉打擾您召喚假摔哥，有找您的電話。」

"I'm sorry to interrupt you when you're summoning the Yatsuhakamura, but there is a call for you."

「經理，抱歉打擾您召喚八墓村的亡靈，有找您的電話。」

"I'm sorry to interrupt you when you're summoning the assistant manager, but there is a call for you."

「經理，抱歉打擾您召喚副理，有找您的電話。」

"I'm sorry to interrupt you when you're summoning a pond snail, but there is a call for you."

「經理，抱歉打擾您召喚田螺，有找您的電話。」

CHAPTER 2

考試不會出現的
英文會話

10 NONESSENTIAL CONVERSATIONS

選出最不貼近商務和日常生活，
使用起來最不麻吉的10則會話練
習。要朗讀時請先確認周圍沒有
其他人，且儘量小聲背誦就好。

001

A wonderful Safari Park

Stefanie: Hi, Kate! I heard you went to the Safari Park last weekend. How was it?

Catherine: It was fantastic! We saw lions and underwear thieves, right in front of our eyes. Those wild animals really wound me up.

Stefanie: Underwear thieves? That sounds great!

Catherine: In the Safari Park, we can hand-feed the animals. In fact, I was quite scared when I gave my panties and bras to the underwear thieves.

Stefanie: Wow! So you can actually feed them? I think I should go there with my boyfriend.

Catherine: You have to go! It's more exciting than watching them on TV!

好棒的野生動物園

史蒂芬妮：嗨，凱特！我聽說妳上週末去了野生動物園，好玩嗎？

凱薩琳：太好玩了！在妳眼前會出現活生生的獅子和內衣小偷唷！野生動物真的太令人興奮了啦！

史蒂芬妮：內衣小偷？聽起來真棒耶！

凱薩琳：在野生動物園可以直接餵食，但要拿內褲和奶罩餵內衣小偷時還是會覺得有些可怕！

史蒂芬妮：超殺的！真的可以餵食嗎？那我也要找我男朋友一起去。

凱薩琳：妳一定要去！絕對比在電視上看到的內衣小偷更有魄力喔！

【**不重要單字**】underwear thief［名］：內衣小偷／panty［名］：內褲‧「形」：像內褲般的／bra［名］：奶罩(brassiere的縮寫)

 本園正在舉辦與內衣小偷面對面的攝影活動，還有可以親手抱內衣小小偷的互動喔！

002

Receptionist Work

Nick: Hi, Catherine, what are you doing?

Catherine: Hi, Nick, can't you tell? I'm chain-sawing the Ferrari in half.

Nick: Wow! Being a receptionist seems tough.

Catherine: Well, I guess you could say so. It is a worthwhile job, though. After this, I'll grind them into a powder, and eventually the company will release it as "Ferrari Powder".

Nick: "Ferrari Powder"? What's it for?

Catherine: Well, it's supposed to be used as a digestive medicine. The active substances of the luxury car are modestly effective for weak stomachs, poor circulation, and fatigue.

Nick: Hmmm…That's amazing. I can't wait to see it! Ah, I think someone's at the door.

Catherine: Oh, may be the Pope. Damn! Why is everybody bothering me?

總機小姐的工作

尼克：嗨，凱薩琳。妳在做什麼？

凱薩琳：嗨，尼克。你是目瞜糊到蜆仔肉嗎？

我正在用電鋸把法拉利切成兩半！

尼克：天啊，櫃台總機的工作還真不輕鬆呀！

凱薩琳：還好啦。

之後還要用銼刀把車子磨成粉，做成「法拉利之粉」拿去賣。

尼克：法拉利之粉？那要怎麼用？

凱薩琳：拿來做胃腸藥。高級進口車的有效成分對於腸胃虛弱的人、手腳發冷、容易疲勞的人都很有效。

尼克：哇，太厲害了！好令人期待喔！ㄟ，好像有客人來了。

凱薩琳：唉，應該是羅馬教宗。討厭，進度一直卡住！

【不重要單字】chain-saw［自他動］：用電鋸切割／Ferrari［人名］：法拉利／digestive medicine［名］：胃腸藥／Pope［名］：羅馬教宗(慣用：the Pope、Pope）

 使用「法拉利之粉」前請仔細閱讀說明。
即使遵照用法和劑量來正確使用，仍然會有危險。

003

President's Lips

Bob: Nick! How is he doing right now?

Nick: Well, he is in the Intensive Care Unit and has been placed on a ventilator. The doctor says, we are not allowed to see him now.

Bob: Ventilator! That worries me. I heard he suddenly collapsed during his meal and was rushed to hospital by ambulance.

Nick: Yes, he has been suffering from chapped lips for a long time. He shouldn't have eaten that Big Mac.

Bob: No, he shouldn't have, but that's just how he is.

Nick: According to the CT scan, his lips have been deeply wounded.

Bob: Recently, his lips have been seriously dry and rough. I had a feeling something like this might happen.

Nick: Well, the doctor says, with an early operation, he could leave the hospital with no after effects. I say he'll be OK.

Bob: That's a relief. If it were a heart bypass operation, I'd do it myself!

Nick: Stop blowing your own trumpet!

總裁的嘴唇

鮑伯：尼克，總裁的病情如何了？

尼克：嗯啊，現在正在加護病房治療中，裝了人工呼吸器，並謝絕訪客探視。

鮑伯：人工呼吸器？真令人擔心！

聽説他是用餐時突然倒下，被救護車送去醫院的？

尼克：嗯，很久之前他就已經嘴唇乾裂，

結果居然還吃大麥克，真是不該吃的！

鮑伯：原來如此……但很像是總裁的作風呀！

尼克：照了嘴唇的電腦斷層掃瞄，好像裂得非常地深。

鮑伯：最近總裁的嘴唇很乾裂，我就覺得一定會出事的説。

尼克：醫生説只要儘早動手術就不會留下後遺症，一定沒問題的啦！

鮑伯：這樣我就放心了。如果要動心導管手術，可以找我開喔！

尼克：別再吹牛了！

【**不重要單字**】ventilator［名］：通風孔、換氣裝置、人工呼吸器／chapped lips［名］：嘴唇粗糙、嘴唇乾裂／Big Mac［名］：大麥克(熱量547大卡)

 乾裂的地方只要塗上護唇膏，放著就會自己好的説。

004

A call

Catherine: The Teiai Foundation, good morning. How may I help you?

Bush: Good morning. This is Mr. Bush from Mugen Ltd. calling for Mr. Mushanokoji.

Catherine: I'm sorry. We have 37 Mr. Mushanokojis here. Masaru or Naruhiko or Ryu or Kyoichi…

Bush: OK, just a moment…ah…I think he belongs to the advertising department.

Catherine: I see. One moment please. I'll put you through to Mr. Mushanokoji.

Catherine: Boss, I'm sorry to interrupt you while you're creating a magic barrier. There is a call for you.

Mushanokoji: Hi Catherine, thank you. Who's calling?

Catherine: Mr. Bush from Mugen Ltd.

Mushanokoji: Mm…Tomorrow is Butsumetsu, so I have to get this done today. Let me call him back later.

Catherine: I see. I'll let him know.

Mushanokoji: Wait, Catherine!

Catherine: Yes?

Mushanokoji: Can you bring me a Prayer Ring from the general affairs department?

電話

凱薩琳：早安。這裡是諦愛基金會，請問有什麼事嗎？

布希：早安。敝人是無限公司的布希，麻煩替我轉接武者小路先生。

凱薩琳：不好意思，敝社有37位武者小路，優、成彥、龍、恭一……

布希：呃，請等一下，我記得他好像是宣傳部的。

凱薩琳：了解，請稍等，現在就替您轉接武者小路。

凱薩琳：經理，抱歉在設下結界中打擾您，有電話找您。

部長：喔，凱薩琳，謝謝。是誰打來的？

凱薩琳：無限公司的布希先生。

部長：是嗎？明天是佛滅日，我希望能在今天前弄好，
請轉告我會再回電給他。

凱薩琳：明白了，我會轉告他的。

部長：等一下，凱薩琳！

凱薩琳：什麼事？

部長：去總務那邊幫我拿祈禱之戒過來。

【**不重要單字**】magic barrier［名］：結界／Prayer Ring［名］：祈禱之戒(恢復魔法點數20～30MP，用了幾次就會崩壞)

 宣傳部門製作這結界是用來防小人還是防什麼？

Marketing Department

Stefanie: Hello, Nick! I heard the marketing department is looking for a work-ready masochist. Are you thinking of applying?

Nick: Of course I am. Actually, I am quite interested in masochism. But I'm worried about whether I can make it in the department. There are too many serious perverts over there.

Stefanie: No need to be modest. You're such a flasher. In that area of business, no-one can touch you!

Nick: You flatter me! I still have a lot to learn.

Stefanie: Anyway, I think you should talk to your director. He's one of the most famous perverts in our company.

Nick: Sounds good! I'll talk to him when he comes back from the gangbang.

Stefanie: Really? It's still the middle of the day. He never fails to amaze me!

Nick: He's a reliable man. Plus, he is a keen scatologist, gangbanger, and paedophile. A three-point pervert, I say.

Stefanie: I wonder why he hasn't been fired yet.

行銷部門

史蒂芬妮：哈囉，尼克。行銷部好像要找一個馬上就能派上用場的被虐待狂，你有興趣試試嗎？

尼克：當然有！其實我對當受虐狂非常有興趣，但是我擔心能不能在行銷部門表現良好，那裡有太多厲害的變態了！

史蒂芬妮：你就別謙虛了。只要提到暴露狂，沒有人比得上你！

尼克：別捧我了，我的毛都還沒長齊呢！

史蒂芬妮：總之，你應該先去找課長商量一下，他是我們公司中最有名的變態。

尼克：好的！等我從雜交派對回來後就去找他。

史蒂芬妮：天啊，現在是大白天耶！你真是嚇到我了。

尼克：課長是個可靠的人，而且還是屎屎愛好狂、濫交達人、戀童癖，簡直是三位一體的完美變態！

史蒂芬妮：為什麼他還沒有回家吃自己，真是想不透啊！

【不重要單字】masochist[名]：被虐待狂・[形]：自虐的／masochism[名]：受虐狂、自我虐待／flasher[名]：自動閃光裝置、暴露狂／pervert[名]：性倒錯、變態／gangbang[名]：雜交派對／scatologist[名]：屎屎愛好狂／paedophile[名]：戀童癖・[形]：戀童癖的

 只溶你手、亂入OK、隨你把玩，三位一體的超級玩家！

006

In the bathroom(1)

Clerk: Good evening. Do you have a reservation?

Bob: No.

Clerk: How many in your party, sir?

Bob: 4.

Clerk: How about a seat at the counter?

Bob: Why not the table?

Clerk: Unfortunately, the tables are full at the moment. We will have to ask you to wait.

Bob: How long is the wait?

Clerk: About thirty minutes.

Bob: Well, I already have a turtlehead. OK, we'll take a seat at the counter.

Clerk: Thank you. Japanese-style or western-style?

Bob: Western-style please.

Clerk: Would you like open front type or oval type?

Bob: Open front type, please.

洗手間(1)

店員：歡迎光臨,請問有預約嗎?

鮑伯：沒有。

店員：請問有幾位呢?

鮑伯：4位。

店員：給你們安排在吧台的位子可以嗎?

鮑伯：沒有餐桌區嗎?

店員：抱歉,現在餐桌座位全滿了,必須要等一會兒才有。

鮑伯：要等多久?

店員：大約30分鐘。

鮑伯：不行,便便快出來了,就坐吧台好了!

店員：謝謝您的諒解。請問要日式還是西式?

鮑伯：西式的。

店員：請問要U型還是O型?

鮑伯：U型好了。

【不重要單字】have a turtle［俗］：便便快出來了／Japanese-style［名‧形］：日式／western-style［名‧形］：西式／open front style［名‧形］：U型(便座)／oval style［名‧形］：O型(便座)

 幸好不是和陌生人坐在一起。

007

In the bathroom(2)

Clerk: Which kind of toilet paper would you like?

Bob: Elleair, please.

Clerk: How would you like your paper done?

Bob: Medium-rare, please.

Clerk: When would you like to have your paper? Before the defecation? Or after?

Bob: After , please.

Clerk: Certainly. This way please…Enjoy your defecation.

Bob: Excuse me? Bill, please.

Clerk: Sure. Here you are.

Bob: Can I pay by credit card?

Clerk: Sure. Do you have a T-point card?

Bob: No.

Clerk: Thank you very much. We are looking forward to seeing you again!

Bob: Thank you. Oh, sorry, could we have a doggie bag?

洗手間(2)

店員：衛生紙的種類要選哪一種？

鮑伯：五月花。

店員：衛生紙要幾分熟的？

鮑伯：五分熟就好。

店員：衛生紙要什麼時候上？排便前？還是排便後？

鮑伯：排便後。

店員：了解，請往這邊。請好好享受您的排便。

鮑伯：不好意思，我要結賬。

店員：好的，這是您的消費金額。

鮑伯：可以刷卡嗎？

店員：可以的。請問有集點卡嗎？

鮑伯：沒有。

店員：謝謝您的惠顧，歡迎下次再來。

鮑伯：不客氣。對了，我可以要一個打包袋嗎？

【 **不重要單字** 】MAY FLOWER［品名］：五月花／defecation［名］：排便／doggie bag［名］：打包袋

 打包回去是想幹什麼？

008

In a Church

Priest: Trusty sweatshop servant, what do you seek at our church?

AAAA: I'd like to resurrect the personnel manager.

Priest: That requires a donation of 7 gold. Is that okay?

AAAA: No.

Priest: Mercy! Donations to the church show gratitude towards God. How pathetic of you to be so stingy. Can I do anything else for you?

AAAA: I'd like to resurrect the vice personnel manager.

Priest: That requires a donation of 5 gold. Is that okay?

AAAA: Yes.

Priest: Do you have a T-point card?

AAAA: No.

Priest: Would you like a new card?

AAAA: No.

Priest: Almighty God! If it is your will, please resurrect the sweatshop servant, and the vice personnel manager!

(The vice personnel manager returns to life!)

AAAA: May I have a receipt, please?

在教堂

神父：忠誠黑心企業的僕人，汝為了何目的來到教堂？

路人甲：請求上帝讓人事經理復活。

神父：這樣的話請奉獻7枚金幣給本教會，汝可以嗎？

路人甲：做不到。

神父：天殺的！奉獻是表達對神的感謝之意，居然吝於付出，太不敬了！
其它還有什麼請求嗎？

路人甲：請求上帝讓副理復活。

神父：這樣的話請奉獻5枚金幣給本教會，汝可以嗎？

路人甲：好的。

神父：汝有TSUTAYA集點卡嗎？

路人甲：沒有。

神父：要辦一張新卡嗎？

路人甲：不用了。

神父：全知全能的主啊！
請賜給忠誠黑心企業的僕人——讓副理的靈魂來到他的身邊！

（副理復活了）

路人甲：請問有收據嗎？

【**不重要單字**】sweatshop［名］：壓榨勞工的企業、黑心企業／resurrect［他動］：讓人復活／T-point card［品名］：TSUTAYA集點卡

 那人事經理的死活就沒人管了嗎？

009

Christie's operation(1)

Christie: Pulse rate, blood pressure, and anal pressure are all normal. The patient's power level is 530000.

Dr. Williams: Good. Let's start the lip-suture operation.

Christie: OK. So first, take a deep breath… and hold it.

Dr. Williams: Christie, this is not an X-ray examination, it's an operation. Just pass me a scalpel.

Christie: Here you are.

Dr. Williams: Christie, not a urine bottle. A scalpel, please.

Christie: Here you are.

Dr. Williams: All right. Well, lip, lip…

Christie: Doctor, that isn't a lip, it's a nipple.

Dr. Williams: Whoops! Well…this?

Christie: Doctor, that isn't a lip, it's the duodenum.

Dr. Williams: Dammit! Well…here?

Christie: That's the anus. Are your eyes open? You are going down and down.

Dr. Williams: I'm not quite myself today. Let's take a break now. Could you make some coffee?

Christie: Sure, doctor.

克莉絲蒂的手術體驗（1）

克莉絲蒂：脈搏數正常、血壓正常、肛壓正常，病患的戰鬥力是53萬。

威廉：好，現在開始嘴唇縫合手術。

克莉絲蒂：好，首先深呼吸……好，停住！

威廉：克莉絲蒂，現在不是照X光，是在動手術！把手術刀給我。

克莉絲蒂：好的，這個。

威廉：克莉絲蒂，不是尿壺，是手術刀！

克莉絲蒂：好的，這個。

威廉：嗯，嘴唇在哪～

克莉絲蒂：醫生，那裡不是嘴唇，是乳頭。

威廉：喔，搞錯了，是這個吧？

克莉絲蒂：醫生，那不是嘴唇，是十二指腸。

威廉：哎呀，又搞錯了，是這裡嗎？

克莉絲蒂：醫生，那是肛門！你目睭糊到蜆仔肉嗎？愈摸愈下面了啦！

威廉：今天的狀況很瞎，休息一下好了。妳可以幫我泡個咖啡嗎？

克莉絲蒂：好的，醫生。

【**不重要單字**】power level［名］：戰鬥力／suture［名］：縫合・［他動］：進行縫合／scalpel［名］：手術刀／urine bottle［名］：尿壺／duodenum［名］：十二指腸

 既然都要縫合傷口了，為什麼還要動用手術刀？

010

Christie's operation(2)

Christie: Doctor, enough Mario Kart, let's resume surgery.

Dr. Williams: Yeah. Let's get going…Damn! No way…

Christie: What's the matter?

Dr. Williams: I accidentally spilled some coffee on the patient.

Christie: No problem. I'll wipe it off.

Dr. Williams: Thank you, but I spilled it on his face, not his anus.

Christie: Oh, dear. I was careless. Oh?

Dr. Williams: What now?

Christie: Doctor, I see macadamia nuts all over his duodenum.

Dr. Williams: Woops! I've left his stomach open.

Christie: No problem. I'll vacuum it.

Dr. Williams: Be careful. Only vacuum the nuts.

Christie: No problem. I might not look so, but I'm a psychopath.

Dr. Williams: That's not the point and this isn't the duodenum, it's the anus.

Christie: Woops.

克莉絲蒂的手術體驗 (2)

克莉絲蒂：醫生，瑪利歐賽車就先打到這好了，繼續進行手術吧！

威廉：也對，來開刀吧！啊，靠！

克莉絲蒂：怎麼了？

威廉：不小心把咖啡灑在患者身上了。

克莉絲蒂：沒事，我來擦掉就好。

威廉：多謝了。不過灑到的地方不是肛門，是在臉上。

克莉絲蒂：喔，我好像太謹慎了。呃？

威廉：又怎麼了？

克莉絲蒂：醫生，我看到很多夏威夷豆掉在患者的十二指腸上了。

威廉：慘了，他的肚子還剖開著！

克莉絲蒂：沒問題，我用吸塵器把它們吸掉！

威廉：小心點，只要把豆子吸掉就好！

克莉絲蒂：沒問題啦！別看我這樣，我可是一個精神病患者呢！

威廉：這不是重點！那裡不是十二指腸，是肛門啦！

克莉絲蒂：唉呀！

【不重要單字】Mario Kart[品名]：瑪利歐賽車／anus[名]：肛門／macadamia nuts[名]：夏威夷豆／psychopath[名]：精神病患者

 醫生，搞笑可不可以到此為止，病人在等著你開刀啊！

不想唸出聲的英文單字
Words you don't want to read out loud.

各位如果有想要實現的夢想和願望，不妨寫在紙上把它們唸出來，說不定話語的力量就能讓夢想實現喔！

語言有靈（the soul of language），所以說出來的話很有可能就會照著內容實現，世上就是有這種神奇的力量。你不信嗎？

那麼以下例句請用丹田的力量，在公眾場合大聲唸出來。你一定會感受到什麼叫做言語的力量！

It's a big areola. You can't miss it.
那麼大的乳暈，你不可能看不到的！

☞ 當有人向你問路時，在替他指路後不妨再加上這一句，
　　保証對方一定會被你弄得很混亂的！

This nipple is different from what I expected!
這和我想的乳頭不一樣！

☞ 做愛時，當你解下胸罩的釦環，請用丹田的力量大聲說。
　　保証讓你有個激烈難以忘懷的夜晚。

A flat-chest is the best defence.
貧乳是最大的防禦。

☞ 當心儀的男性看到妳的胸部後立馬喪鬥志時，別忘了要火冒三丈的大聲說！
　　保証他會照著妳的心戰喊話重拾「性」趣的。

If we don't end fake boobs, fake boobs will end us.
如果我們不終結假奶，假奶就會終結我們。

☞ 你可以混進反核武運動的人群中，大聲說出一呼百諾；
　　保証對反核沒有興趣的男人就會一一前來連署。

I can't blame him. He's a pervert.
我無法譴責他，因為他是個變態。

☞ 看到有人被斥責時，不妨悄悄上前去說出這句，
　　保証就會獲得原諒了。

There is still so much to be learned about F-cups.
關於F罩杯仍有太多的未解之謎。

☞ 你可以嗆聲那些敢說自己很了解的人，
　　保証他們立刻就會為自己的無知感到汗顏。

Everyone! Your bowel movement isn't over until you wipe your bottom.
各位！排便完要擦了屁股才算數！

☞ 在廁所前面大聲疾呼，
　　保証很多人又會再進去重上一次。

CHAPTER 3

考試不會出現的
長文解讀

10 NONESSENTIAL LONG TEXTS

「留言」、「行程」、「廣告」，
這些都是在商務範疇中看起來能
派上用場的主題，在此嚴選10
則極其做作且糟蹋內容的長文
章，要是您在文脈中不自覺就能
記住單字和片語，那真是再糟糕
也不過了。

001

Office Message

TO: Okamoto Toshihiro

FROM: Saito Tetsuko

TIME: 10：45, Monday

Telephone - Fax - Office Visit - Carrier Pigeon - (Telepathy)

Priority: High

Subject: Change of rendezvous location

Message:

There was a telepathic message

from Saito Tetsuko your sex slave.

She wants to change the rendezvous location

because Hotel Casablanca's rooms are too small

to jump on each other.

Can you see her at Hotel Brown Bullet instead?

She also mentioned

she would love to be gagged tonight.

Please call her back telepathically as soon as

you get back from the gangbang.

Taken By: Takahashi Yoshiko

公司留言

To：岡本俊宏 先生

From：齊藤哲子 小姐

時間：星期一 **10:45**

電話 · 傳真 · 親訪 · 信鴿 · 心電感應

優先度：高

主旨：更改會面地點

留言：

有一通來自性奴隸齊藤哲子小姐的心電感應。

因為卡薩布蘭加旅館的房間太小不適合玩性遊戲，

在此想要更改會面地點。

如果是改到褐色彈丸旅館會面可行嗎？

還有，她說今晚嘴巴想含口球束具。

如果你從雜交派對回來，

請儘快用心電感應回覆她。

留言者：高橋芳子

【不重要單字】Carrier Pigeon［名］：信鴿／sex slave［名］：性奴隸／rendezvous［名］：會面、會面場所／gag［名］：含口球束具·［他動］：讓人含上口球束具／gangbang［名］：雜交派對

 如此清楚的留言，輕易地就將公私混為一談。

002 Ransom Letter

Dear Kozuke Zoo

We have your zookeeper.

If you want to see HIM again, prepare fifty million yen by tomorrow.

If you fail to do so, he'll be dead meat.

Also, we unwittingly have your koala as well.

If YOU want to breed him again, prepare three large bags of eucalyptus leaves by tomorrow.

If you fail, he'll be dead meat. You can't expect a kidnapper to have eucalyptus leaves.

Don't tell the cops anything.

If we find any cops at the drop-off point, negotiations are over.

Also, don't tell the fierce animals anything.

If we find any lions or tigers at the DROP-OFF point, negotiations are over.

Only if you follow the instructions do WE guarantee their safety and nutrition.

We will call you again tomorrow. You can hear from them then.

Once again, please make sure you don't say anything to the fierce animals.

This is not a joke.

PS

Hippopotamuses count as fierce animals as well.

恐嚇信

敬告 上野 動物 園

貴 園 的 餵食 工作 人員 在 我的 手上。

如果 想要 再 見他 一面，明天 之前 準備好 5 千萬。

沒有 準備好 的話，餵食人員 將 性命不保。

還有，貴園 的 無尾熊 也 不小心 落在 我們 手上。

如果 想 要再 餵養 牠，

明天 之前 準備好 三大袋 裝滿 尤加利 樹葉 的 袋子。

如果 沒有 準備 好，無尾熊 也 將 性命 不保。

你 不能 期望 綁架犯 手上 會有 尤加利 樹葉。

不准通知 警察！

如果 付款 地點 出現 警察 的 蹤影，交涉 就立刻 決裂！

還有 不准 告訴 猛 獸！

如果 付款 地點 出現 猛獸 的 身影，交涉 立刻 視為 破裂。

只要 乖乖 遵照 我 的指示 去做，

就 可保証 他們 的 性命 和營養 無虞。

明天會 再 打電話 通 知。

到 時，會 讓 你們 聽見 他們 的 聲音。

再 提醒 一次，絕對 不可以 讓 猛獸 知道。

沒有 在 開 玩笑 的！

附 注

河馬 也包括 在 猛獸 之中！

【不重要單字】eucalyptus［名］：尤加利樹／kidnapper［名］：綁架犯／drop-off point［名］：付款地點／hippopotamus［名］：河馬

 不知猩猩是否也算是猛獸呢？

003

The origin of the G-cup (1)

G-cups. The dream of every male. Currently, it is said that the percentage of women with G-cups living in Japan is less than 1%. They inhabit many parts of Japan, though mainly reside in the Tohoku region. However, nobody knows precisely where they came from.

People in the past thought that women with G-cups were imaginary creatures. In the murals of the Kofun period, you can find people worshiping women with G-cups as God. Also, some archaeologists say that Himiko of Yamatai-koku had a G-cup. "The twinborn G-cups" statue inside the Tenjinyama tomb in the city of Ota, Gunma Prefecture is designated as a national treasure.

G罩杯的起源（1）

G罩杯。這是所有男人夢寐以求的。

現在，據說棲息在日本G罩杯的比例大約是1%以下。

以東北地方為中心，廣泛分布在日本全國之中。

事實上G罩杯是從哪裡來的，

迄今還是完全不清楚。

在古早時代，

G罩杯被認為是不存在的生物。

古墳時代的壁畫中，

畫著G罩杯被人們尊崇為神明的場景。

另外，也有考古學者主張

邪馬台國的卑彌呼女王有G罩杯。

位於群馬縣太田市天神山墓地的

「雙子G罩杯像」已經被指定為國寶。

【**不重要單字**】G-cup［名］：G罩杯／mural［名］：壁畫／tomb［名］：墳墓、墓地

 對於缺乏營養的古代人而言，豐滿的胸圍只應天上有吧！

004

The origin of the G-cup (2)

Throughout history, there were times when women with G-cups were feared to be devils rather than the work of God. In the middle of the Heian period, they were seen as a threat to the power of the Fujiwara-clan. Fujiwara-no-Dio, who is known as a flat-chest maniac, persecuted the women with G-cups severely. Women with G-cups feared for their life, so they tied their kimono sashes around their chest very tightly, and had to live in secret. Those so called "Crypto G-cups" were subjected to severe punishment when the government found them out.

After the Meiji government was established in 1868, women with G-cups were free and now they are loved by all, from children to adults. One of Japan's largest G-cup festivals is held in the city of Ota, Gunma Prefecture. Approximately 1,000,000 big boob lovers come from all over the country to join.

G罩杯的起源(2)

回顧歷史，G罩杯的存在一度造成恐慌，

被認為不是神明的偉業，而是惡魔在作祟。

平安時代中期，

G罩杯的存在被認為將威脅到藤原氏的權力，

身為貧乳控的藤原泥男進行了大規模的迫害。

感受到殺身之禍的G罩杯紛紛用纏胸布束胸，

並藏身在不為人知之處。

她們被稱做「祕密的G罩杯」，

一旦被政府發現就會遭受嚴厲的懲罰。

1868年隨著明治政府的成立，

G罩杯終於又恢復自由之身，

如今已是大人小孩都愛不釋手的寵兒。

群馬縣太田市每年舉辦一次

日本最大型的G罩杯祭典，

約有100萬的G罩杯愛好者從各地蜂擁而來。

【**不重要單字**】flat-chest maniac［名］：貧乳控／sash［名］：窗櫺、帶子、纏胸布／crypto［形］：祕密的・［名］：祕密結社

 現代的G罩杯可說是伴隨明治時代的進代化一路發展下來的。

005

TEIAI Group 2013 Joint Orientation schedule for new employees

April 1, 2013

* Initiation Ceremony
* Welcome Speech by Mr. Samuel L Mushanokoji (CEO's second cousin)
* Introduction of Board Members and their mistresses
  Place: Central Office
  Welcome Party: Marathon (42.195km)

April 2, 2013

* Company Guidance
  Mr. Suizo Chikubi (Part-time Staff)
* Taking Photograph for ID Card (removal of clothing) / Collection of fingerprints / Branding with a hot iron / Stamping with blood
  Place: Central Office Basement
  Social gathering: Marathon (42.195km)

April 3, 2013

* Induction Course 1
  Business Manner
  Instructor Mr. X
  (Masked Sales Department)
  how to greet customers / how to answer the telephone / how to use honorific expressions / how to hand out business cards / how to trade hostages / how to enter the ring / how to push bunt / how to use a dragon radar
  Place: Mt.Hakkoda
  Recreation: Marathon (42.195km)

April 4, 2013

* Induction Course 2
  Mind Control (OJT)
  Holy Master Mr.Michel Phowa
  how to find weak points / how to hold on to weak points / how to hit weak points / how to aggravate anxieties / how to drive to despair / how to create God
  Place: The room of spirit and time
  Barbecue Party: Marathon (42.195km)

April 5, 2013

* Induction Course 3 Survival
  Instructor Ms.Catherine WRYYYYYYYYYY Brando (receptionist)
  how to bow hunt / how to set traps / how to find edible plants / how to use guns / how to escape from bears
  Place: Gunma Prefecture
  Bowling Party: Marathon (42.195km)

April 6, 2013 - March 31, 2020

* Forced Labor
  Place: the Pacific

April 1, 2020 -

* Temporary Posting

諦愛集團 2013 新進員工研習時間表

2013 年 4 月 1 日
* 開幕式
* 歡迎致辭
  山繆‧L‧武者小路氏
  （CEO的姪子的姪子）
* 董事們和小三的介紹

  地點：總公司
  歡迎會：馬拉松大會（42.195公里）

2013 年 4 月 2 日
* 公司概要説明
  乳頭吸允氏（打工人員）
  ID卡人像拍照（必須全裸）
  採集指紋‧烙印‧蓋血指印

  地點：總公司地下室
  親睦會：馬拉松大會（42.195公里）

2013 年 4 月 3 日
* 2013 年 4 月 2 日
  研習 1 商務禮儀講座
  講師Mr.X氏（偽裝營業部）
  打招呼方式‧電話應對方式
  敬語的使用‧名片交換方式
  人質交換方式‧上擂台的方式
  觸擊的揮棒方式
  尋龍雷達的使用方法

  地點：八甲田山
  娛樂活動：馬拉松大會（42.195公里）

2013 年 4 月 4 日
* 研習 2 心神控制
  （實地演練）宗師　麥可勃啊氏
  找出弱點的方法‧掌握弱點的方法
  擊破弱點的方法‧煽動不安的方法
  給予絕望的方法‧造神的方法

  地點：精神時光屋
  B.B.Q派對：馬拉松大會（42.195公里）

2013 年 4 月 5 日
* 研習 3 絕境求生
  講師　凱薩琳‧無力
  布蘭多（櫃台人員）
  弓箭狩獵方法‧陷阱設置方法
  辨試可食用草的方法
  槍的使用方法‧遇到熊時的逃跑方法

  地點：群馬縣
  保齡球大會：馬拉松大會（42.195公里）

2013 年 4 月 6 日
~2020 年 3 月 31 日
* 強制勞動
  地點：太平洋

2020 年 4 月 1 日
* 暫時分發

【不重要單字】mistress［俗］：小三／Collection of fingerprints［片‧名］：採集指紋／brand with a hot iron［片‧動］：烙印／Stamp with blood［片‧動］：蓋血指印／hostage［名］：人質／push bunt［名］：觸擊／dragon radar［名］：尋龍雷達／Holy Master［名］：宗師／The room of spirit and time［名］：精神時光屋／Forced Labor［名］：強制勞動

note! 黑心企業果然讓連鎖餐飲業也自嘆不如啊！

006

HERO WANTED!

Are you STRONG enough?
Are you MAGICAL enough?
Are you BRAVE enough?

We are looking for a hero who would like to save the world. The working hours are long, and the risk of death is extremely high. However, if you manage to achieve your goal, you will be rewarded with world-wide acknowledgement and fame. Stand up friend! The whole world is waiting for you!

Job Description
It is an easy assignment to stop the Great Satan's evil ambitions and save all humanity.
Working hours: 24 hours a day, 7 days a week
Work location: The whole world(including the Lower World)
Employment period: Until you defeat the final boss

Skills, qualifications and experience required
Human only (no monsters)
Advanced swordsmanship and high magical capacity.
Good communication skills
Experience in defeating low level monsters (Eg. Slime, Drakee)
Tolerance for the grotesque
Driver's license (manual license required.)

Offers
Salary: Commission based.
Supplied uniform: Wayfarer's clothes
Welfare: Unlimited usage of the Church resurrection system.
Transportation: Horse cart supplied.

For more information,
please e-mail Nishimura at luidas_bar@gmail.com
Don't miss this chance to be a legend

勇者募集

你有好體力嗎？
你會唸咒語嗎？
你有真勇氣嗎？

我們正在尋找想要拯救世界的勇者，
勇者必須長時間勞動，甚至有丟掉性命的危險；
一旦成功就能獲得全世界人的感謝，贏得美名讚譽。
來，奮起吧！世界正等著你來拯救！

工作內容
阻止魔王的邪惡野望以拯救人類，工作內容單純。
出勤時間：一天24小時，一週7天
勤務地點：全世界（含地下世界）
雇用期間：直到打倒最後老大為止

必要的能力、資格、經驗
限定人類（謝絕怪物）
高超劍術與魔法的能力
良好的溝通能力
具有弱小怪物的討伐經驗（史萊姆、德拉奇）
耐異形屬性
普通駕照（必須有操作手冊）

待遇
薪俸：基本傭金
制服配給：旅人之服
福利醫療：可無限使用教會的死後復活
交通：備有馬車
詳情請電郵詢問西村 luidas_bar@gmail.com
千萬不要放棄成為傳說的機會！

【不重要單字】Slime［名］：史萊姆／Drakee［名］：德拉奇／tolerance for the grotesque［名］：耐異形屬性

 居然還有Gmail信箱？

A new "Learn to Knit" Workshop will be starting soon!

Nancy Smith presents

"Knit your own barbed wire workshop"

Nancy is an ex-army engineer
and an excellent barbed wire knitter.
Her classes are usually filled to capacity.
She'll teach you the basic stitches,
how to cast on and off, and some handy hints
to make your barbed wire look wonderful!

No skills required

This workshop is designed for beginners.
We will start from square one
and teach all the basic barbed wire knitting techniques.

Iron wires will be included in the kit.
There will be refreshments available.
(hot & cold drinks, Band-Aids, ointments).

Come join us and knit your own barbed wire!

全新編織工作坊即將開幕！

跟南西・史密斯一起學

編織有刺鐵絲工作坊

南西・史密斯是前陸軍工兵隊員，
是一位手巧的有刺鐵絲編織達人。
她的講座總是場場爆滿。
她會從開始著手到完成編織，教導基本的手法，
還會讓妳學到如何把有刺鐵絲編得完美的竅門。

無需必要技術

本工作坊適合初學者，
我們會從基礎開始，
教導你所有有刺鐵絲的處理方式和編織技巧。

鐵絲會由工作坊準備教材，
另備有輕食（果汁、OK繃、軟膏）。

快來加入我們編出屬於你的美好鐵絲吧！

【不重要單字】barbed wire［名］：有刺鐵絲／start from square one［片］：從基礎開始／Band-Aid［名］：OK繃／ointment［名］：軟膏

 讓我們用誠心來做出刺進肉裡的尖銳鐵絲吧！

How to cook a barium steak

Ingredients

200g	barium meal
1/2	onion
1	egg
1/2 cup	bread crumbs
2 tablespoons	milk
1 tablespoon	ketchup
1 tablespoon	Worcestershire sauce
1/4 cup	Blue Hawaii syrup

Salt / pepper / house dust
Vegetable oil
Benz powder
Laxatives

Directions

1. Chop onion finely and sauté it well in the vegetable oil.
2. Put the egg, milk and bread crumbs in a bowl and stir it.
3. Take off all your clothes.
4. Add the barium meal and cooked onion. Use your whole body to mix it up.
5. Put on your bras.
6. Add some salt, pepper and house dust.
7. Separate the patty into two. Then summon your STAR PLATINUM and let it make a well in the center of the patties.
8. Heat the oil in a large pan and sauté the patties on a medium heat with your eyes closed.
9. Flip the patty and sauté the other side. Add 1/4 cup of Blue Hawaii syrup to the pan and cover with the lid and steam the patty for few minutes.
10. Remove the patty from the pan, and add ketchup, Worcestershire sauce, Benz powder to the empty pan. Then cook it for 30 seconds.
11. Pour the sauce over the barium patties and put on your panties.

*After eating, get an X-ray exam and take a laxative.

鋇漢堡的製作方法

材料

鋇	200 公克
洋蔥	1/2 個
雞蛋	1 個
麵包粉	1/2 杯
牛奶	2 大匙
蕃茄醬	1 大匙
伍斯特醬	1 大匙
藍色夏威夷	1/4 杯
鹽、胡椒、家裡灰塵	
植物油	
粉末狀的賓士	
瀉藥	

調理說明

1. 將洋蔥切碎，用植物油炒過。
2. 將雞蛋、牛奶、麵包粉倒入碗中，仔細攪拌。
3. 將衣服全部脫光。
4. 加進鋇、炒好的洋蔥，並用全身用力的攪拌。
5. 穿上胸罩。
6. 加入鹽、胡椒、家裡灰塵
7. 麵糊分成兩等份，發動白金之星，將中間打凹。
8. 在大的平底鍋中熱油，閉起眼睛用中火煎。
9. 翻面再煎，倒進藍色夏威夷後蓋上鍋蓋，悶煎漢堡幾分鐘。
10. 將漢堡起鍋，加上蕃茄醬、伍斯特醬、賓士粉末，再用火烤 30 秒。
11. 將鋇漢堡醮醬並穿上內褲。

※吃完後請去做 X 光檢查，並喝下瀉藥。

【不重要單字】barium［名］：鋇／Blue Hawaii syrup［名］：藍色夏威夷（剉冰的糖漿）／house dust［名］：家裡灰塵／Benz［品名］：賓士／laxative［名］：瀉藥／STAR PLATINUM［人名］：白金之星

 不敢吃鋇的人有口福了！

009

Train Announcement
(Tsurumai Electric Railway, Yagibushi Line)

This is the Yagibushi line train bound for Nise-Takasaki and Kiryu In-The-Sky.

The next station is Yakimanju. The doors on the right side will open. Please change here for the Sugiki-Mozaemon subway line.

There are priority seats in each carriage. Please give up these seats for flat-chested passengers, shut-ins, falsely pregnant mothers and passengers accompanying a designated hitter.

The next station is Negi & Konyaku. The doors on the both sides will open. Please change here for the Shiden-Shimonita line, and the Nuclear Test subway line.

Please switch off your pacemaker when you're near the priority seats, and in other areas, please set it to stop mode and refrain from pulsing. Thank you for your cooperation.

Tsurumai Electric Railway and Yellow-Cab are now both on high alert. If you find any suspicious fake boobs at a station or on a train, please inform the station staff, conductors or security guards as soon as possible.

車內廣播
（鶴舞電鐵 八木節線）

本電車是繞行八木節線內圈，開往偽高崎・桐生in the sky方向。

下一部是燒饅頭，燒饅頭。出口是右側車門。

本站可換乘杉木茂左衛門線。

本電車設有博愛座位，如有貧乳和長期自閉在家的乘客、

帶著假想懷孕或指定打者的乘客，

請讓座給他們。

下一站是蔥和蒟蒻，蔥和蒟蒻。出口是兩側車門。

本站可轉乘市電下仁田線、地下鐵核實驗線。

在博愛座附近請將心律調整器的電源關掉。

在車廂內其它地方請調到停止模式，避免心臟的跳動。

感謝您的體諒與協助。

現在鶴舞電鐵和小黃互相合作，實施特別警戒。

車站內和電車內如有發現可疑的假奶時，

請儘速向站員和警衛通報。

【不重要單字】flat-chested［形］：貧乳的／shut-in［名］：長期自閉在家／falsely pregnant［名］：假想懷孕／designated hitter［名］：指定打者／pacemaker［名］：心律調整器／Yellow-Cab［名］：小黃／fake boobs［名］：假奶

 note! 哎呀，飛機場小姐，妳請坐。

Self Promotion

Good morning, I'm Stefanie Pantyline Mifune. I currently work as a temporary employee's body double in the air-raid shelter of a Japanese-affiliated company. Sexiness and agility are my biggest strong points. All my employees, friends, dolphin trainers and dolphins have said I am sexy and fast. I am so-called the "Sonic Nipple." I also have a tough anus and excellent anti-aircraft defense. I can catch a Patriot missile with my anus.

I have an autistic personality, yet cheerful at the same time. I am a taurine-rich Bakufu supporter but I am also a psychotic, which makes me different from a Zaku. I am different from a Zaku. I am a natural born leader, and I served as prison leader during my student days. I also won the Best Jean-wearer prize in the Talent Scout Caravan held by the temple of Dhama.

Of course, I've never even been hit by my father.

Since my supervisor is not human, my role is to act as a mediator between him and hundreds of ghouls. In addition to my routine work, I make Clara stand, and then set Clara down, and make Clara stand again, and then set Clara down. The supervisor is probably one of the most competent perverts in our punishment cell, so he is nicknamed "Samurai with Erotic Eyes". I learned a lot about the "Longzhong Plan" from him.

Since I read "2channel" and found out that your company is not a sweatshop, I'm looking forward to join you. With my "Stand" ability which I acquired through training in the Amazon, I'd like to help Clara execute a belly roll.

自我推薦

　　大家早安。我是史蒂芬妮・內褲線。現在在日資企業的防空洞中當派遣社員的影武者。我的優點是性感和動作快。同事和朋友、海豚訓練師和海豚都說我既性感又動作快，所以幫我取了「音速乳頭」這個外號。還有，肛門很強韌，具有高度對空防禦力，並能用肛門接住愛國者飛彈。

　　我的性格有點自閉、為人快活，體內含豐富的牛磺酸，支持幕府者。我同時是精神障礙者，因此和札克不一樣，我就是和札克不一樣。我是一個天生的領導者，學生時代擔任過牢房班長，參加達瑪神殿主辦的大型選秀活動，獲得最佳牛仔褲穿著獎。還有，我從來沒有被爸爸打過。

　　因為現在的上司不是人類，我的工作就是在他與數百隻食屍鬼之間進行溝通。還有，在平常的業務之外，還要幫克拉拉大小姐站起來、幫克拉拉大小姐坐下去；又要幫克拉拉大小姐站起來、又要幫克拉拉大小姐坐下去。上司恐怕是我在懲罰房中最不廢柴的一位變態，他被叫做「色瞇瞇的武士」。我在他手下學習到很多有關三分天下之計。

　　我有先上2ch（日本網路論壇）查過貴公司並不是黑心企業，所以很希望可以加入你們。希望將來能發揮在亞馬遜河學到的替身（幽波紋）能力，幫助克拉拉大小姐用腹滾翻跳高。

【不重要單字】body double[名]：影武者／air-raid shelter[名]：防空洞／Sonic Nipple[綽號]：音速乳頭／Patriot missile[名]：愛國者飛彈／autistic[形]：自閉的／taurine[名]：牛磺酸／Bakufu supporter[名]：支持幕府者／psychotic[形]：獵奇的、精神有問題的・[名]：精神障礙者／Zaku[品名]：札克／prison leader[名]：牢房班長／Talent Scout Caravan[名]：大型選秀活動／temple of Dhama[名]：達瑪神殿／ghoul[名]：咕嚕、盜墓者、食屍鬼／punishment cell[名]：懲罰房／Samurai with Erotic eyes[名]：色瞇瞇的武士／LongZhong plan[名]：三分天下之計／stand[名]：替身(幽波紋)／belly roll[名]：腹滾翻

 錄用！

附加例句集
Extra Phrases

A罩杯 A-cup
例句 Mr.Suzuki emphasized why A-cups are more attractive than F-cups.
鈴木氏解說為什麼A奶比F奶對男人更有魅力的理由。

不穿內褲 no underwear
例句 No underwear is advisable, but not compulsory.
勸導不穿內褲,但不強制執行。

即位登基 assume the throne
例句 "All those who collect five stamps can assume the throne!"
「集滿五枚印花,就可即位登基!」

液態史萊姆 Liquid Metal Slime
例句 "How many times do I have to tell you? Don't use magic on the Liquid Metal Slime!" Zhuge Liang yelled.
「到底要我說幾次!不要對液態史萊姆使用咒語!」諸葛亮大吼道。

女用燈籠褲 bloomers
例句 "Nowadays there are only a few real perverts who take bloomers seriously."
「最近認真肖想穿女用燈籠褲的變態
只剩下極少數一撮人。」

音速的 sonic
例句 Some colleagues call Stefanie the "Sonic Nipple".
有好幾位同事都叫史蒂芬妮是「音速乳頭」。

聽診器 stethoscopes
例句 Doctors practiced swinging and breaking the stethoscopes for the academic conference.
醫生們用學會準備的聽診器練習揮舞,並且拉扯。

開高衩 high-cut leg
例句 High-cut legs look best from a distance.
拉開距離看開高衩才好看。

手銬 handcuffs
例句 These handcuffs are great for both police and criminals.
這副手銬是警察和犯人同時都可以享受樂趣的。

伊娜鮑爾 Ina Bauer
例句 From October 1st, doing an Ina Bauer on the road will be banned in Adachi Ward, Tokyo.
10月1日開始,東京都足立區禁止在路上做伊娜鮑爾的動作。

孫子兵法 Sun-tzu's Art of War
例句 Zhuge Liang accidentally dropped Sun-tzu's Art of War in the toilet.
諸葛亮不小心把孫子兵法掉在茅坑中了。

網子 net
例句 Ten years ago, our president found Bob entangled in a net off the coast, and brought him back to the office.
10年前,總裁在海岸邊發現了被網子纏住的鮑伯,就把他帶回來公司。

CHAPTER 4

考試不會出現的看圖說故事

35 NONESSENTIAL PICTURE OF PRACTICES

每張圖會標出4則短文。選出最能「適切符合」圖中的狀況和登場人物心理的其中一則敘述,並且要裝出自己很用功的樣子。只要裝得非常用功就更能顯現出拚命三郎的模樣。

Practice
001

(A) She is sinking her teeth into a Rolls-Royce.
她在啃勞斯萊斯轎車。

(B) She is plucking her pubic hair.
她在拔陰毛。

(C) She is shouldering the napalm bomb.
她扛著汽油彈。

(D) She is expressing her urge to pee without saying a word.
她不說一語卻能表現出尿急。

Practice
002

(A) My brother has been watching "Charlie's Angels"
ever since he received a heavy blow to the head.
弟弟自從被大力K到頭後，就一直在看《霹靂嬌娃》。

(B) My brother has been pitching root crops ever since he received a heavy blow to the head.
弟弟自從被大力K到頭後，就一直在投根莖類蔬菜。

(C) My brother has been observing the slugs ever since he received a heavy blow to the head.
弟弟自從被大力K到頭後，就一直在觀察蛞蝓。

(D) My brother has been touching his groin ever since he received a heavy blow to the head.
弟弟自從被大力K到頭後，就一直在摸鼠蹊部。

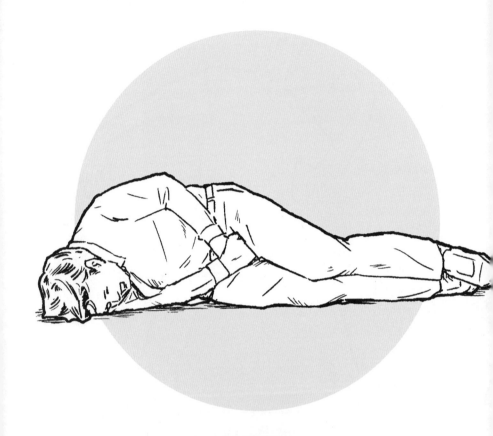

Practice
003

(A) He seemed as if somebody had stepped on his temple on the train this morning.
他今早在電車上被人踩到了太陽穴。

(B) He seemed as if somebody had stepped on his Adam's apple on the train this morning.
他今早在電車上被人踩到了喉結。

(C) He seemed as if somebody had stepped on his nipple on the train this morning.
他今早在電車上被人踩到了乳頭。

(D) He seemed as if somebody had stepped on his groin on the train this morning.
他今早在電車上被人踩到了鼠蹊部。

(A) He is Audrey Hepburn.
他是奧黛莉赫本。

(B) He is soaking his anus in warm water, our foreman is taking a short break from work.
把肛門浸泡在溫水裡,我們的工頭終於可以喘口氣了。

(C) Guntank missed White Base by a minute.
鋼坦克以毫釐之差錯過了白色基地。

(D) "Don't touch the floor. I've just finished the pomade coating."
「不要碰地板,我剛才打上了髮油。」

Practice 005

(A) The man is joking, but feeling horny at the same time.
他一直搞笑，同時還想嘿咻。

(B) Guntank pretended he didn't see Gundam just pass him.
鋼坦克和鋼打姆擦身而過，卻假裝沒看到他。

(C) All the parsley you can eat for 3,000 yen.
3000日幣就可享用荷蘭芹吃到飽。

(D) You are required to participate in the midmorning "high heel fight" session, but are free to do what you like in the afternoon.
上午要參加互丟高跟鞋會議，下午就可以自由活動。

**Practice
006**

(A) Yesterday, my mom was showing off her Nunchuck prowess,
but today she is feeding the pigeons.
阿母昨天還很威風的在耍雙節棍，今天卻裝優雅在餵鴿子。

(B) Yesterday, my mom was showing off her Nunchuck prowess,
but today she is flat on her back in the hospital.
阿母昨天還很威風的在耍雙節棍，今天卻躺在醫院病床上。

(C) The Governor of the Bank of Japan was given a direct red card for a vicious sliding tackle.
日銀總裁因為惡意的剷人，立刻遭到紅牌出場。

(D) Nick ate some cardboard boxes, and then asked Stefanie to marry him.
尼克吃了幾個紙箱後，開口要求史蒂芬妮嫁給他。

Practice
007

(A) The woman is twirling the knickerbockers.
那女人在揮舞著燈籠褲。

(B) The Marie Antoinette are arranged in a circle.
瑪麗安東娃妮特排成一個圓圈。

(C) Contrary to our expectations, the manager's fart has continued for more than two hours.
出乎我們的意料，經理的屁一直放了2個小時。

(D) The rice cooker is playing an instrument.
電鍋正在演奏樂器。

(A) Do viagra tablets count as a snack?
點心裡要加威而鋼嗎？

(B) Our annual company policy is "No magic."
敝公司今年的目標是「不准使用咒語」。

(C) I would like to send five boxes of assorted blunt instruments as a midyear gift.
今年中元節想送五盒鈍器的禮盒。

(D) Bob is pinching his nipple to signify his disagreement.
鮑伯捏著乳頭以表達他的不贊成意見。

Practice
009

(A) The man is pouring whipped cream over some dumbbells.
    那男人在啞鈴上抹了一些奶油。

(B) The man is scattering curry powder to the wind.
    那男人在空中撒了一些咖哩粉。

(C) The man loves G-cups, but G-cups don't love him.
    那男人喜歡G奶,但G奶不甲意他。

(D) The man was planning to show Ken his uvula, but changed his mind.
    那男人本來要讓肯看他的懸雍垂,但現在改變心意了。

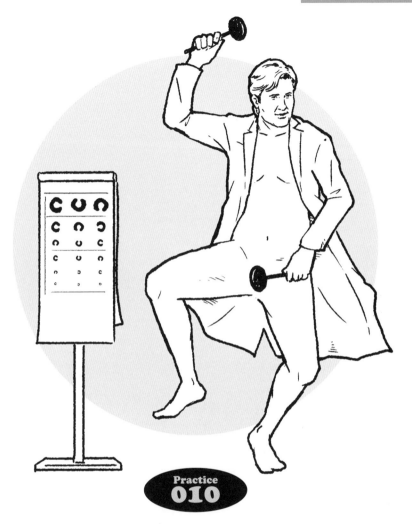

Practice
010

(A) The man is trying to soothe the baby's crying by dancing the lambada.
那男人跳著黏巴達，希望讓哭鬧的嬰兒安靜下來。

(B) In Gunma Prefecture, trapezes are used for education and administration.
在群馬縣，在教育和行政上都會使用高空鞦韆。

(C) The ophthalmologist is performing "The Occluder Dance" at the year-end party.
那個眼科的驗光師在尾牙上跳著「遮眼板之舞」。

(D) To mark the start of the ceremony, the chairperson struck a naked bridge pose.
主席用裸體表演裸體鐵板橋姿勢，宣告典禮要開始了。

解答 001～010

001

(A) She is sinking her teeth into a Rolls-Royce.
她在啃勞斯萊斯轎車。

(B) She is plucking her pubic hair.
她在拔陰毛。

(C) She is shouldering the napalm bomb.
她扛著汽油彈。

(D) She is expressing her urge to pee without saying a word.
她不說一語卻能表現出尿急。

［正解］D

【 不重要單字 】Rolls-Royce：勞斯萊斯／pubic hair：陰毛／napalm bomb：汽油彈
☞ 淑女的矜持。

002

(A) My brother has been watching "Charlie's Angels"
ever since he received a heavy blow to the head.
弟弟自從被大力K到頭後，就一直在看《霹靂嬌娃》。

(B) My brother has been pitching root crops ever since he received a heavy blow to the head.
弟弟自從被大力K到頭後，就一直在投根莖類蔬菜。

(C) My brother has been observing the slugs ever since he received a heavy blow to the head.
弟弟自從被大力K到頭後，就一直在觀察蛞蝓。

(D) My brother has been touching his groin ever since he received a heavy blow to the head.
弟弟自從被大力K到頭後，就一直在摸鼠蹊部。

［正解］B

【 不重要單字 】Charlie's Angels：霹靂嬌娃／root crop：根莖類蔬菜／slug：蛞蝓
／groin：鼠蹊部
☞ 工作人員接到投出來的根莖類蔬菜都說很美味。

003

(A) He seemed as if somebody had stepped on his temple on the train this morning.
他今早在電車上被人踩到了太陽穴。

(B) He seemed as if somebody had stepped on his Adam's apple on the train this morning.
他今早在電車上被人踩到了喉結。

(C) He seemed as if somebody had stepped on his nipple on the train this morning.
他今早在電車上被人踩到了乳頭。

(D) He seemed as if somebody had stepped on his groin on the train this morning.
他今早在電車上被人踩到了鼠蹊部。

［正解］D

【 不重要單字 】temple：太陽穴／Adam＇s apple：喉結

☞ 會被踩到的橫躺姿勢才是最大的問題！

004

(A) He is Audrey Hepburn.
他是奧黛莉赫本。

(B) He is soaking his anus in warm water, our foreman is taking a short break from work.
把肛門浸泡在溫水裡，我們的工頭終於可以喘口氣了。

(C) Guntank missed White Base by a minute.
鋼坦克以毫釐之差錯過了白色基地。

(D) "Don't touch the floor. I've just finished the pomade coating."
「不要碰地板，我剛才打上了髮油。」

［正解］B

【 不重要單字 】Audrey Hepburn：奧黛莉赫本／White Base：白色基地
／pomade：髮油

☞ 站著工作很傷肛門，要好好休息才行。

005

(A) The man is joking, but feeling horny at the same time.
他一直搞笑，同時還想嘿咻。

(B) Guntank pretended he didn't see Gundam just pass him.
鋼坦克和鋼打姆擦身而過，卻假裝沒看到他。

(C) All the parsley you can eat for 3,000 yen.
3000日幣就可享用荷蘭芹吃到飽。

(D) You are required to participate in the midmorning "high heel fight" session,
but are free to do what you like in the afternoon.
上午要參加互丟高跟鞋會議，下午就可以自由活動。

［正解］A

【 不重要單字 】horny：想嘿咻／parsley：荷蘭芹／high heels：高跟鞋

☞ 這是最恐怖的類型：賣笑又賣身。

006

(A) Yesterday, my mom was showing off her Nunchuck prowess, but today she is feeding the pigeons.
阿母昨天還很威風的在耍雙節棍，今天卻裝優雅在餵鴿子。

(B) Yesterday, my mom was showing off her Nunchuck prowess,
阿母昨天還很威風的在耍雙節棍，
今天卻躺在醫院病床上。

(C) The Governor of the Bank of Japan was given a direct red card for a vicious sliding tackle.
日銀總裁因為惡意的剷人，立刻遭到紅牌出場。

(D) Nick ate some cardboard boxes, and then asked Stefanie to marry him.
尼克吃了幾個紙箱後，開口要求史蒂芬妮嫁給他。

［正解］B
【不重要單字】Nunchuck：雙節棍／sliding tackle：剷人

☞ 可能是玩太大了！希望她能早日康復，從精神病院被放出來。

007

(A) The woman is twirling the knickerbockers.
那女人在揮舞著燈籠褲。

(B) The Marie Antoinette are arranged in a circle.
瑪麗安東娃妮特排成一個圓圈。

(C) Contrary to our expectations, the manager's fart has continued for more than two hours.
出乎我們的意料，經理的屁一直放了2個小時。

(D) The rice cooker is playing an instrument.
電鍋正在演奏樂器。

［正解］C
【不重要單字】Knikcerbocker：燈籠褲／Marie Antoinette：瑪麗安東娃妮特／fart：屁

☞ 放出來的應該已經不是瓦斯，而是什麼咒術了吧？

008

(A) Do viagra tablets count as a snack?
點心中要加威而鋼嗎？

(B) Our annual company policy is "No magic."
敝公司今年的目標是「不准使用咒語」。

(C) I would like to send five boxes of assorted blunt instruments as a midyear gift.
今年中元節想送五盒鈍器的禮盒。

(D) Bob is pinching his nipple to signify his disagreement.
鮑伯捏著乳頭以表達他的不贊成意見。

［正解］D

【不重要單字】viagra：威而鋼／no magic：不准使用咒語／blunt instrument：鈍器
／nipple：乳頭

☞ 捏→不贊成、彈→贊成、蓋住→保留、拿起→謝罪、飛走→開戰。

009

(A) The man is pouring whipped cream over some dumbbells.
那男人在啞鈴上抹了一些奶油。

(B) The man is scattering curry powder to the wind.
那男人在空中撒了一些咖哩粉。

(C) The man loves G-cups, but G-cups don't love him.
那男人喜歡G奶，但G奶不甲意他。

(D) The man was planning to show Ken his uvula, but changed his mind.
那男人本來要讓肯看他的懸雍垂，但現在改變心意了。

［正解］B

【不重要單字】curry powder：咖哩粉／G-cups：G奶／uvula：懸雍垂

☞ 燕雀安知鴻鵠之志，他肯定是有什麼偉大的企圖。

010

(A) The man is trying to soothe the baby's crying by dancing the lambada.
那男人跳著黏巴達，希望讓哭鬧的嬰兒安靜下來。

(B) In Gunma Prefecture, trapezes are used for education and administration.
在群馬縣，教育和行政上都會使用高空鞦韆。

(C) The ophthalmologist is performing "The Occluder Dance" at the year-end party.
那個眼科的驗光師在尾牙上跳著「遮眼板之舞」。

(D) To mark the start of the ceremony, the chairperson struck a naked bridge pose.
主席用裸體表演裸體鐵板橋姿勢，宣告典禮要開始了。

［正解］C

【不重要單字】lambada：黏巴達／trapeze：高空鞦韆／occluder：遮眼板
／naked bridge：裸體鐵板橋

☞ 這是眼科自古相傳的傳統舞蹈。如果你以為遮眼板只能遮上面的眼，那你可就太小看它了。

(A) The man is not entirely sure where the anus is.
那個男人不確定肛門在哪裡。

(B) This type of medical technologist won't hand his gastroscope to others once he grabs it.
他是那種只要一拿到胃鏡就死也不放手的醫檢師。

(C) "Saggy Tits" mean "peace" in English.
「下垂奶」在英文中代表「和平」的意思。

(D) "I'd like to start from where we left off yesterday. Give me the scalpel."
「我們從昨天停下來的地方重新開始，請給我手術刀。」

(A) "Why did the flat-chest choose me?"
「為什麼貧乳會發生在我身上？」

(B) Next episode "School swimsuits are on the verge of extinction. Save our earth."
Don't miss it!
下一回是「學校泳衣的滅絕危機！保衛我們的地球！」敬請期待。

(C) The fake Santa Claus is lying on the side of the road, covered with chicken nuggets.
冒牌聖誕老人倒在路邊，身上布滿了雞塊。

(D) No need to fear the minefield because we are going to walk together.
只要大家一起，走過地雷區並沒有什麼可怕的。

Practice
013

(A) "Honey, do you know where my glasses are?" "Oh, no, my dear..."
「孩子的媽，有沒有看到我的眼鏡？」「討厭，親愛的…」

(B) "Honey, do you know where my brass knuckles are?" "Oh, no, my dear..."
「孩子的媽，有沒有看到我的手指虎？」「討厭，親愛的…」

(C) "Honey, do you know where my protective cup is?" "Oh, no, my dear..."
「孩子的媽，有沒有看到我的護蛋罩杯？」「討厭，親愛的…」

(D) "Honey, do you know where my tear gas is?" "Oh, no, my dear..."
「孩子的媽，有沒有看到我的催淚瓦斯？」「討厭，親愛的…」

(A) They are flying through the air on a Dyson.
他們跨上戴森飛天而去。

(B) Let's skip the formalities. Please take a dump.
生硬的客套話就不說了，請大家排便吧！

(C) The department manager developed a new sexual position by watching the colour printer closely.
部門經理盯著彩色印表機時，想到了新的體位姿勢。

(D) You are the famous alto recorder, aren't you?
你就是那個很會吹的中音直笛手嗎？

Practice
015

(A) "There's no way you can eat those bloomers!" "That's what you think."
「女用燈籠褲不能吃啊！」「那是你單方面這麼認為。」

(B) "Dad, will your ultimate weapon be free to use next Saturday?"
「爹地，下禮拜六你的最終兵器可以借我用嗎？」

(C) "Come on, Stef, use your turd well."
「來，史蒂芬妮，妳要學會好好運用大便。」

(D) "Calm down, Bob! Ok, first of all, let's put panties on each other."
「放輕鬆，鮑伯！首先，要互相替對方穿上內褲。」

(A) "Have you drawn up the proposal?" "Boss, that isn't the section head. It's a ganglion cyst." "Oops."

「提案寫好了嗎？」「老闆，那個不是課長，是肌腱瘤啦！」「靠！」

(B) People in the Gunma prefecture skillfully use green onions and konjacs as weapons during battles.

在戰鬥中，群馬縣的人民很巧妙地用大蔥和蒟蒻當做武器。

(C) My migratory locust got into trouble for knocking up the female next door.

我家的公蝗蟲讓隔壁的母蝗蟲懷孕引起了糾紛。

(D) The cockroach looks mature but it's only three months old.

這隻蟑螂看起來很成熟，其實只有3個月大。

Practice
017

(A) "Excuse me, but your kidney is showing." "Oops."
「不好意思，你的腎臟跑出來了。」「歹勢。」

(B) "Why don't you come to your senses and wipe your arse?"
「你可不可以清醒一點把屁股給擦了？」

(C) "May I have your nipple?"
「我可以借看一下你的乳頭嗎？」

(D) He is whispering words of love to her anus.
他對著她的屁眼訴說愛的絮語。

(A) "Don't give up. Cling to hope till the very end. The game isn't over till you wet your pants."
「不要放棄最後的希望！只要一尿溼褲子比賽就結束囉！」

(B) "What does this 'JSA' stand for?" "Jet Stream Attack."
「這個JSA是什麼的簡稱？」「Jet Stream Attack.」

(C) "Oh, if only I had some chloroform..."
「靠，要是有氯仿（三氯甲烷）就好了……」

(D) "Thank God, tomorrow's Friday." Frieza said wistfully.
「感謝龍神，明天終於星期五了。」弗利沙碎碎念道。

(A) Bob has no real knowledge of what it's like to be busty.
鮑伯根本就不了什麼是真正的巨乳。

(B) "Could you explain this pubic hair to me?"
「你能解釋一下這根陰毛嗎？」

(C) Some G-cups are poisonous.
有些G奶是有毒的。

(D) Bob looked at the G-cup boobs, but they turned their nipples away from him.
鮑伯直盯著G奶看，但G奶把乳頭撇過去不給他看。

Practice
020

(A) "Oops, sorry. How silly of me. This is the pope."
「喔，抱歉，我昏頭了。這位是羅馬教宗。」

(B) "You have big areolas. What's your secret?" "Sorry, it's confidential."
「好大的乳暈啊，請問有什麼祕訣嗎？」「抱歉，這是機密。」

(C) My parents don't approve of my new fuck buddy.
我的父母不認同我的新炮友。

(D) "I couldn't understand that. Could you pinch my nipples?"
「我有聽沒有懂。你可以捏著我的乳頭說嗎？」

解答 011～020

011

(A) The man is not entirely sure where the anus is.
那個男人不確定肛門在哪裡。

(B) This type of medical technologist won't hand his gastroscope to others once he grabs it.
他是那種只要一拿到胃鏡就死也不放手的醫檢師。

(C) "Saggy Tits" mean "peace" in English.
「下垂奶」在英文中代表「和平」的意思。

(D) "I'd like to start from where we left off yesterday. Give me the scalpel."
「我們從昨天停下來的地方重新開始，請給我手術刀。」

［正解］A
【不重要單字】medical technologist：醫檢師／gastroscope：胃鏡／saggy tits：下垂奶

☞ 但凡世間事物皆無定數，更何況是小小肛門的位置。

012

(A) "Why did the flat-chest choose me?"
「為什麼貧乳會發生在我身上？」

(B) Next episode "School swimsuits are on the verge of extinction. Save our earth." Don't miss it!
下一回是「學校泳衣的滅絕危機！保衛我們的地球！」敬請期待。

(C) The fake Santa Claus is lying on the side of the road, covered with chicken nuggets.
冒牌聖誕老人倒在路邊，身上布滿了雞塊。

(D) No need to fear the minefield because we are going to walk together.
只要大家一起，走過地雷區並沒有什麼可怕的。

［正解］A
【不重要單字】flat-chest：貧乳／school swimsuits：學校泳衣／minefield：地雷區

☞ 上天既然選中了妳，就要挺胸而行！

013

(A) "Honey, do you know where my glasses are?" "Oh, no, my dear..."
「孩子的媽，有沒有看到我的眼鏡？」「討厭，親愛的…」

(B) "Honey, do you know where my brass knuckles are?" "Oh, no, my dear..."
「孩子的媽，有沒有看到我的手指虎？」「討厭，親愛的…」

(C) "Honey, do you know where my protective cup is?" "Oh, no, my dear..."
「孩子的媽，有沒有看到我的護蛋罩杯？」「討厭，親愛的…」

(D) "Honey, do you know where my tear gas is?" "Oh, no, my dear..."
「孩子的媽，有沒有看到我的催淚瓦斯？」「討厭，親愛的…」

［正解］B

【不重要單字】brass knuckles：手指虎／protective cup：護蛋罩杯／tear gas：催淚瓦斯

☞ 待會要去決鬥嗎？現在不能再裝傻了！

014

(A) They are flying through the air on a Dyson.
他們跨上戴森飛天而去。

(B) Let's skip the formalities. Please take a dump.
生硬的客套話就不說了，請大家排便吧！

(C) The department manager developed a new sexual position by watching the colour printer closely.
部門經理盯著彩色印表機時，想到了新的體位姿勢。

(D) You are the famous alto recorder, aren't you?
你就是那個很會吹的中音直笛手嗎？

［正解］B

【不重要單字】Dyson：戴森（吸塵器）／take a dump：排便／alto recorde：中音直笛手

☞ 打起精神提「肛」挈領，不然就要漏出來了！

015

(A) "There's no way you can eat those bloomers!" "That's what you think."
「女用燈籠褲不能吃啊！」「那是你單方面這麼認為。」

(B) "Dad, will your ultimate weapon be free to use next Saturday?"
「爹地，下禮拜六你的最終兵器可以借我用嗎？」

(C) "Come on, Stef, use your turd well."
「來，史蒂芬妮，妳要學會好好運用大便。」

(D) "Calm down, Bob! Ok, first of all, let's put panties on each other."
「放輕鬆，鮑伯！首先，要互相替對方穿上內褲。」

［正解］A

【不重要單字】bloomer：女用燈籠褲／ultimate weapon：最終兵器／turd：大便

☞ 若是否定自我的可能性，那真是連神都幫不上忙了。

016

(A) "Have you drawn up the proposal?" "Boss, that isn't the section head. It's a ganglion cyst." "Oops."
「提案寫好了嗎？」「老闆，那個不是課長，是肌腱瘤啦！」「靠！」

(B) People in the Gunma prefecture skillfully use green onions and konjacs as weapons during battles.
在戰鬥中，群馬縣的人民很巧妙地用大蔥和蒟蒻當做武器。

(C) My migratory locust got into trouble for knocking up the female next door.
我家的公蝗蟲讓隔壁的母蝗蟲懷孕引起了糾紛。

(D) The cockroach looks mature but it's only three months old.
這隻蟑螂看起來很成熟，其實只有3個月大。

［正解］C

【不重要單字】ganglion cyst：肌腱瘤、腱鞘囊腫／konjac：蒟蒻／migratory locust：公蝗蟲

☞ 養子不教誰之過？要怎麼收穫，先那麼栽。

017

(A) "Excuse me, but your kidney is showing." "Oops."
「不好意思，你的腎臟跑出來了。」「歹勢。」

(B) "Why don't you come to your senses and wipe your arse?"
「你可不可以清醒一點把屁股給擦了？」

(C) "May I have your nipple?"
「我可以借看一下你的乳頭嗎？」

(D) He is whispering words of love to her anus.
他對著她的屁眼訴說愛的絮語。

［正解］C

【不重要單字】kidney：腎臟／arse：屁股／anus：屁眼

☞ 請看。

018

(A) "Don't give up. Cling to hope till the very end. The game isn't over till you wet your pants."
「不要放棄最後的希望！只要一尿溼褲子比賽就結束囉！」

(B) "What does this 'JSA' stand for?" "Jet Stream Attack."
「這個JSA是什麼的簡稱？」「Jet Stream Attack.」

(C) "Oh, if only I had some chloroform..."
「靠，要是有氯仿（三氯甲烷）就好了……」

(D) "Thank God, tomorrow's Friday." Frieza said wistfully.
「感謝龍神，明天終於星期五了。」弗利沙碎碎念道。

［正解］A

【 不重要單字 】Jet Stream Attack：噴射氣流攻擊／chloroform：氯仿(三氯甲烷)／Frieza：弗利沙(漫畫七龍珠的反派角色)

☞ 報告老師，應該是尿出來後再比大小才對吧？

019

(A) Bob has no real knowledge of what it's like to be busty.
鮑伯根本就不了什麼是真正的巨乳。

(B) "Could you explain this pubic hair to me?"
「你能解釋一下這根陰毛嗎？」

(C) Some G-cups are poisonous.
有些G奶是有毒的。

(D) Bob looked at the G-cup boobs, but they turned their nipples away from him.
鮑伯直盯著G奶看，但G奶把乳頭撇過去不給他看。

［正解］C

【 不重要單字 】busty：巨乳的／pubic hair：陰毛／G-cups：G奶

☞ 不好意思，請問G奶到底是什麼可怕的生物？

020

(A) "Oops, sorry. How silly of me. This is the pope."
「喔，抱歉，我昏頭了。這位是羅馬教宗。」

(B) "You have big areolas. What's your secret?" "Sorry, it's confidential."
「好大的乳暈啊，請問有什麼祕訣嗎？」「抱歉，這是機密。」

(C) My parents don't approve of my new fuck buddy.
我的父母不認同我的新炮友。

(D) "I couldn't understand that. Could you pinch my nipples?"
「我有聽沒有懂。你可以捏著我的乳頭說嗎？」

［正解］C

【 不重要單字 】pope：羅馬教宗／areola：乳暈／fuck buddy：炮友

☞ 射人先射馬，擒賊先擒王。理當先介紹給祖父母和兄弟認識才對啊！

Practice 021

(A) Guntank rushed out of White Base in a temper.
鋼坦克火氣一來，就衝出白色基地了。

(B) There is a chronic shortage of big boobs in this company.
這間公司有慢性巨乳不足的毛病。

(C) Our conference room is famous for being the best spot to pick up girls.
敝公司的會議室是有名泡正妹的地方。

(D) The first two days will be devoted to orientation for our incoming new assassins.
頭兩天已經安排了剛進公司新人殺手的教育訓練。

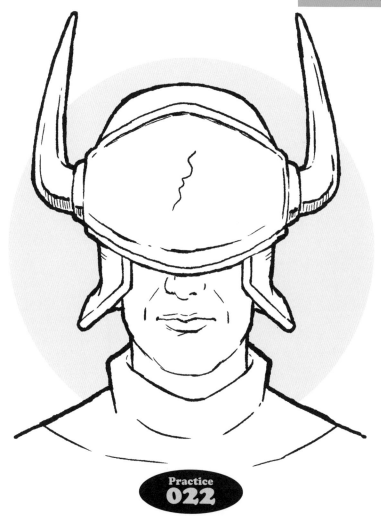

(A) The hero calls it the Emblem of Roto, though it clearly resembles a pubic hair.
勇者把這稱為洛特的徽章，但怎麼看都是根陰毛。

(B) "Where is my Loto's Sword?" "The priest is using it to get the fuzz off his sweater."
「你有看見我的洛特之劍嗎？」「僧侶拿去刮毛衣上的毛了。」

(C) Although this hair-growth drug was successfully tested on our manager,
it is still years away from human use.
這個生髮劑用在我們經理身上的實驗雖然成功了，但要真正用在人體上還得經過好多年。

(D) The conflict between Disneyland and Puroland turned bloody,
costing 38 Kitty Whites' lives.
迪士尼和三麗鷗彼此的對立已演變成了流血事件，死了38隻Kitty。

Practice
023

(A) I hear that a pervert is coming down from Scotland.
變態自蘇格蘭而來。

(B) I hear that a PE teacher is coming down from Scotland.
體育教師自蘇格蘭而來。

(C) I hear that a Namekian is coming down from Scotland.
那美克星人自蘇格蘭而來。

(D) I hear that a masked wrestler is coming down from Scotland.
覆面摔角手自蘇格蘭而來。

(A) "If you show your panties, I can give you a 15 percent discount."
「如果秀內褲給我看，我就幫你打85折。」

(B) "Just for future reference, could you tell me a little bit about your erogenous zone?"
「為了後生晚輩們，可以請教一下你的性感帶的事嗎？」

(C) "Watch out! He's carrying turd!"
「小心！他身上帶屎！」

(D) "This is an emergency. Stay calm and touch your groin."
「緊急情況！大家鎮定，自摸鼠蹊部。」

Practice
025

(A) "Today's guest is Mr.Kim, a secret agent from North Korea. Please give him a big hand!"
「今天的貴客是從北韓來的情報員金先生，請給他一個熱烈的掌聲！」

(B) Though apparently unhealthy, our section chief really has big areolas.
課長雖然看起來一副要死的樣子，但其實有個大乳暈。

(C) "What?! The department manager found a Medicinal Herb!"
「什麼？部門經理找到了藥草！」

(D) "What a waste of big tits!"
「真是白白糟蹋了大奶！」

**Practice
026**

(A) "This underarm hair looks authentic, but actually it's imitation." "Oh, great!"
　　「這腋毛看起來是真的，但其實是仿冒品。」「酷！」

(B) This seductive underwear is for both men and women.
　　這款勝負內褲是男女都可穿的。

(C) "No reply. Must be a shut-in."
　　「沒人應門。一定是自閉在家。」

(D) "No reply. Must be a shapewear."
　　「沒人應門。一定是在穿調整型內衣。」

Practice
027

(A) Three years have passed since the senior staff failed to lay down a sacrifice bunt.
自從資深專員的犧牲觸擊失敗後，轉眼已經過了3年。

(B) "DOM" stands for "Dauntless Obliterator Magnificent".
「DOM」是「偉大不屈抹殺者」的簡稱。

(C) My cat seems to appreciate the value of the Japanese oval gold coin.
我家的貓似乎不理解小金幣的價值。

(D) Out of respect for the manager's hair roots,
all sales department members are not allowed to use the air-conditioning.
為了保護經理的髮根，業務部禁止使用空調。

(A) Elephants have long trunks, rabbits have long ears, and section chiefs have cleft chins.
大象鼻子長，兔子耳朵長，課長下巴裂。

(B) Guncannon came dancing and went away laughing.
鋼加農跳舞而來，又笑著離去。

(C) The deputy director regards his hair roots as a part of his family.
副主任認為髮根是他的家庭成員之一。

(D) The principal's dream is to pave platforms all over the schoolyard.
校長的夢想是把朝會升旗台鋪滿整座操場。

(A) "Fisherman's apron? You know nothing about naked apron style."
「漁夫穿的圍裙？你根本就不了解裸體穿圍裙的真諦！」

(B) "Boss, this isn't the keyhole. It's an anus." "Oops."
「老闆，那裡不是鑰匙孔，是屁眼。」「瞎！」

(C) "Thanks! I could never have wiped my bottom alone."
「還好有你，我自己一個人無法完成擦屁股。」

(D) "You have a wonderful corn on your foot." "Thank you very much. I'm flattered."
「你腳上有個好漂亮的雞眼！」「沒有啦，講得我都不好意思了。」

Practice 030

(A) The fake Donald was found lying on the side of the road, covered with Big Macs.
冒牌當勞被發現倒在路邊，身上蓋滿了大麥克。

(B) I never even thought that my mole hair might shake the U.S. economy.
沒想到我的痣毛會撼動美國經濟。

(C) I think I know this guy, but I can't remember what his areola looked like.
我應該是認識他的，但是看到他的乳暈卻一點印象都沒有。

(D) Eight people voted in favour, five against, and three vomited their food back up.
8人贊成，5人反對，還有3人吐了。

解答 021～030

021

(A) Guntank rushed out of White Base in a temper.
鋼坦克火氣一來，就衝出白色基地了。

(B) There is a chronic shortage of big boobs in this company.
這間公司有慢性巨乳不足的毛病。

(C) Our conference room is famous for being the best spot to pick up girls.
敝公司的會議室是有名泡正妹的地方。

(D) The first two days will be devoted to orientation for our incoming new assassins.
頭兩天已經安排了剛進公司新人殺手的教育訓練。

[正解] B

【不重要單字】big boobs：巨乳／assassin：殺手

☞ 嗯嗯～這似乎也反映出了人事部門的性癖好。

022

(A) The hero calls it the Emblem of Roto, though it clearly resembles a pubic hair.
勇者把這稱為洛特的徽章，但怎麼看都是根陰毛。

(B) "Where is my Loto's Sword?" "The priest is using it to get the fuzz off his sweater."
「你有看見我的洛特之劍嗎？」「僧侶拿去刮毛衣上的毛了。」

(C) Although this hair-growth drug was successfully tested on our manager, it is still years away from human use.
這個生髮劑用在我們經理身上的實驗雖然成功了，但要真正用在人體上還得經過好多年。

(D) The conflict between Disneyland and Puroland turned bloody, costing 38 Kitty Whites' lives.
迪士尼和三麗鷗彼此的對立已演變成了流血事件，死了38隻Kitty。

[正解] A

【不重要單字】Emblem of Roto：洛特的徽章／hair-growth drug：生髮劑

☞ 別管他了！本人應該也察覺到了，只是拉不下臉罷了。

023

(A) I hear that a pervert is coming down from Scotland.
變態自蘇格蘭而來。

(B) I hear that a PE teacher is coming down from Scotland.
體育教師自蘇格蘭而來。

(C) I hear that a Namekian is coming down from Scotland.
那美克星人自蘇格蘭而來。

(D) I hear that a masked wrestler is coming down from Scotland.
覆面摔角手自蘇格蘭而來。

［正解］A

【 不重要單字 】pervert：變態／PE teacher：體育教師／Namekian：那美克星人／masked wrestler：覆面摔角手

☞ 趕快滾回去！

024

(A) "If you show your panties, I can give you a 15 percent discount."
「如果秀內褲給我看，我就幫你打85折。」

(B) "Just for future reference, could you tell me a little bit about your erogenous zone?"
「為了後生晚輩們，可以請教一下你的性感帶的事嗎？」

(C) "Watch out! He's carrying turd!"
「小心！他身上帶屎！」

(D) "This is an emergency. Stay calm and touch your groin."
「緊急情況！大家鎮定，自摸鼠蹊部。」

［正解］C

【 不重要單字 】erogenous zone：性感帶／turd：屎／groin：鼠蹊部

☞ 屎是列在槍炮管制法中的凶器。

025

(A) "Today's guest is Mr.Kim, a secret agent from North Korea. Please give him a big hand!"
「今天的貴客是從北韓來的情報員金先生，請給他一個熱烈的掌聲！」

(B) Though apparently unhealthy, our section chief really has big areolas.
課長雖然看起來一副要死的樣子，但其實有個大乳暈。

(C) "What?! The department manager found a Medicinal Herb!"
「什麼？部門經理找到了藥草！」

(D) "What a waste of big tits!"
「真是白白糟蹋了大奶！」

［正解］B

【 不重要單字 】secret agent：情報員／areola：乳暈／medicinal herb：藥草

☞ 人不可貌相，乳頭不可斗量。

026

(A) "This underarm hair looks authentic, but actually it's imitation." "Oh, great!"
「這腋毛看起來是真的，但其實是仿冒品。」「酷！」

(B) This seductive underwear is for both men and women.
這款勝負內褲是男女都可穿的。

(C) "No reply. Must be a shut-in."
「沒人應門。一定是自閉在家。」

(D) "No reply. Must be a shapewear."
「沒人應門。一定是在穿調整型內衣。」

[正解]D

【不重要單字】underarm hair：腋毛／shut-in：自閉在家／shapewear：調整型內衣

☞ 一定是手腳伸不出來應門吧？

027

(A) Three years have passed since the senior staff failed to lay down a sacrifice bunt.
自從資深專員的犧牲觸擊失敗後，轉眼已經過了3年。

(B) "DOM" stands for "Dauntless Obliterator Magnificent".
「DOM」是「偉大不屈抹殺者」的簡稱。

(C) My cat seems to appreciate the value of the Japanese oval gold coin.
我家的貓似乎不理解小金幣的價值。

(D) Out of respect for the manager's hair roots,
all sales department members are not allowed to use the air-conditioning.
為了保護經理的髮根，業務部禁止使用空調。

[正解]D

【不重要單字】sacrifice bunt：犧牲觸擊／DOM：偉大不屈的抹殺者／Japanese oval gold coin：日本小金幣／hair root：髮根

☞ 國際髮根保護組織（IUCH=International Union for Conservation Hair Roots）指定瀕臨絕種的髮根。

028

(A) Elephants have long trunks, rabbits have long ears, and section chiefs have cleft chins.
大象鼻子長，兔子耳朵長，課長下巴裂。

(B) Guncannon came dancing and went away laughing.
鋼加農跳舞而來，又笑著離去。

(C) The deputy director regards his hair roots as a part of his family.
副主任認為髮根是他的家庭成員之一。

(D) The principal's dream is to pave platforms all over the schoolyard.
校長的夢想是把朝會升旗台鋪滿整座操場。

［正解］A

【不重要單字】cleft chin：下巴裂／Guncannon：鋼加農／hair root：髮根
／platform：朝會升旗台

☞ 這是隨著職位升級而裂開的嗎？還是被劈裂的？需要資格檢定嗎？實在是充滿著不解之謎啊！

029

(A) "Fisherman's apron? You know nothing about naked apron style."
「漁夫穿的圍裙？你根本就不了解裸體穿圍裙的真諦！」

(B) "Boss, this isn't the keyhole. It's an anus." "Oops."
「老闆，那裡不是鑰匙孔，是屁眼。」「瞎！」

(C) "Thanks! I could never have wiped my bottom alone."
「還好有你，我自己一個人無法完成擦屁股。」

(D) "You have a wonderful corn on your foot." "Thank you very much. I'm flattered."
「你腳上有個好漂亮的雞眼！」「沒有啦，講得我都不好意思了。」

［正解］C

【不重要單字】keyhole：鑰匙孔／corn of one's foot：雞眼

☞ 四隻手搞定一個洞。

030

(A) The fake Donald was found lying on the side of the road, covered with Big Macs.
冒牌當勞被發現倒在路邊，身上蓋滿了大麥克。

(B) I never even thought that my mole hair might shake the U.S. economy.
沒想到我的痣毛會撼動美國經濟。

(C) I think I know this guy, but I can't remember what his areola looked like.
我應該是認識他的，但是看到他的乳暈卻一點印象都沒有。

(D) Eight people voted in favour, five against, and three vomited their food back up.
8人贊成，5人反對，還有3人吐了。

［正解］A

【不重要單字】big mac：大麥克／mole hair：痣毛／areola：乳暈

☞ 警察們津津有味的吃著大麥克。

(A) "What nice chain mail!" "Thank you. I knitted it myself."
「好漂亮的鎖子甲！」「沒有啦，我自己編的。」

(B) The mayor tried to circumvent the law to snatch a load of shower caps.
市長鑽法律漏洞，獲得了大量的浴帽。

(C) "Sorry! I accidentally exorcised the evil spirits."
「不好意思，一不小心就把惡靈除掉了。」

(D) With the approach of warmer weather, Christie started to say bizarre things to herself.
隨著天氣暖化，克莉絲蒂開始奇怪的自言自語。

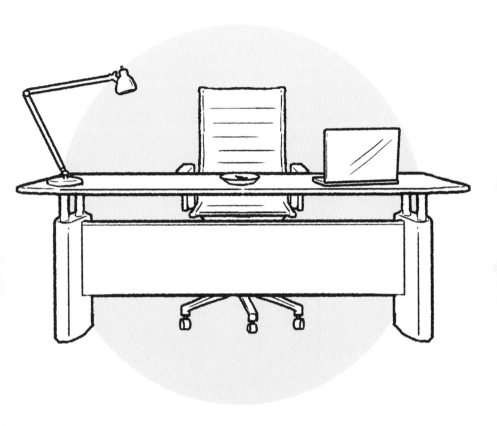

(A) "You idiot! That was Nakajima!"
「笨蛋！那傢伙是中島！」

(B) Indonesia is populated by various big daddies.
在印尼住著形形色色的大人物。

(C) Our senior staff-member must look like a green soybean to an untrained eye, but he is actually human.
在素人眼中看來，我們公司的資深專員像個青豆，其實他是個人。

(D) Gas, electricity and meat juices were cut off due to the disaster.
因為災害的緣故，停止供應瓦斯、電力和肉汁。

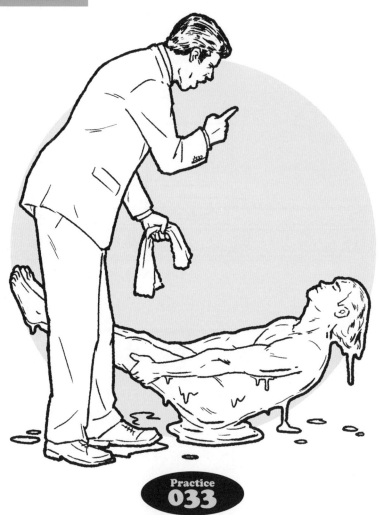

Practice
033

(A) "Bob, will you look after my pubic hair for a couple of minutes?"
「鮑伯，可以請你盯著我的陰毛2~3分鐘？」

(B) "If you don't listen to me, I will remove your slime!"
「如果你不聽我的話，我就要拿走你的黏液！」

(C) "Please urinate anywhere you like."
「請在你中意的任何地方撒尿都行。」

(D) "Let's play house! You'll be Martin Luther and I'll be Fedor Emelianenko."
「我們來玩家家酒，你扮馬丁路德，我扮菲德埃密利亞恩寇。」

(A) Tony the tiger's power level is 530,000.
家樂氏東尼虎的戰鬥力是53萬。

(B) My grandfather takes off his reading glasses whenever he looks at boobs.
祖父在看奶時，一定會摘下老花眼鏡。

(C) His nose hair is standing out conspicuously in the art museum.
他的鼻毛在美術館中特別顯眼。

(D) People thought 30-year old virgins could fly through the air on a broom-stick.
人們認為30歲的童貞可以騎掃把飛天。

(A) Stefanie grabbed Bob's pubic hair and hung on to it for dear life.
史蒂芬妮死命抓住鮑伯的陰毛。

(B) "You've been burning your armpit hair all morning."
"This is part of our new marketing strategy."
「你一整個早上都在燒腋毛。」「這是新的市場行銷戰略的一環。」

(C) "Frieza, your Third Form is not appropriate for a formal party."
「弗利沙，你的第三型態不適合參加正式派對。」

(D) "You can never express your urge to pee in that way."
「你那樣子搞，別人還是不會明白你尿急的。」

解答 031～035

031

(A) "What nice chain mail!" "Thank you. I knitted it myself."
「好漂亮的鎖子甲！」「沒有啦，我自己編的。」

(B) The mayor tried to circumvent the law to snatch a load of shower caps.
市長鑽法律漏洞，獲得了大量的浴帽。

(C) "Sorry! I accidentally exorcised the evil spirits."
「不好意思，一不小心就把惡靈除掉了。」

(D) With the approach of warmer weather, Christie started to say bizarre things to herself.
隨著天氣暖化，克莉絲蒂開始奇怪的自言自語。

［正解］C
【不重要單字】chain mail：鎖子甲／shower cap：浴帽
☞ 送佛送上西天，除靈就用廚房魔術靈。

032

(A) "You idiot! That was Nakajima!"
「笨蛋！那傢伙是中島！」

(B) Indonesia is populated by various big daddies.
在印尼住著形形色色的大人物。

(C) Our senior staff-member must look like a green soybean to an untrained eye, but he is actually human.
在素人眼中看來，我們公司的資深專員像個青豆，其實他是個人。

(D) Gas, electricity and meat juices were cut off due to the disaster.
因為災害的緣故，停止供應瓦斯、電力和肉汁。

［正解］C
【不重要單字】Nakajima：中島／big daddy：大人物／soybean：大豆／meat juice：肉汁
☞ 素人和達人可不只差個人字而已。

033

(A) "Bob, will you look after my pubic hair for a couple of minutes?"
「鮑伯，可以請你盯著我的陰毛2~3分鐘？」

(B) "If you don't listen to me, I will remove your slime!"
「如果你不聽我的話，我就要拿走你的黏液！」

(C) "Please urinate anywhere you like."
「請在你中意的任何地方撒尿都行。」

(D) "Let's play house! You'll be Martin Luther and I'll be Fedor Emelianenko."
「我們來玩家家酒,你扮馬丁路德,我扮菲德埃密利亞恩寇。」

[正解] B

【 不重要單字 】pubic hair:陰毛／slime:黏液／play house:家家酒／Fedor Emelianenko:菲德埃密利亞恩寇(俄羅斯格鬥家)

☞ 居然連黏液都可以當做人質,簡直太卑鄙了!

034

(A) Tony the tiger's power level is 530,000.
家樂氏東尼虎的戰鬥力是53萬。

(B) My grandfather takes off his reading glasses whenever he looks at boobs.
祖父在看奶時,一定會摘下老花眼鏡。

(C) His nose hair is standing out conspicuously in the art museum.
他的鼻毛在美術館中特別顯眼。

(D) People thought 30-year old virgins could fly through the air on a broom-stick.
人們認為30歲的童貞可以騎掃把飛天。

[正解] D

【 不重要單字 】Tony the tiger:家樂氏東尼虎／nose hair:鼻毛

☞ 這是古早時普遍早婚所留下來的傳說。

035

(A) Stefanie grabbed Bob's pubic hair and hung on to it for dear life.
史蒂芬妮死命抓住鮑伯的陰毛。

(B) "You've been burning your armpit hair all morning."
"This is part of our new marketing strategy."
「你一整個早上都在燒腋毛。」「這是新的市場行銷戰略的一環。」

(C) "Frieza, your Third Form is not appropriate for a formal party."
「弗利沙,你的第三型態不適合參加正式派對。」

(D) "You can never express your urge to pee in that way."
「你那樣子搞,別人還是不會明白你尿急的。」

[正解] D

【 不重要單字 】pubic hair:陰毛／armpit hair:腋毛／Frieza:弗利沙

☞ 淑女真不好當耶!即使漏一點出來也無妨吧?

CHAPTER 5

考試不會出現的文法問題

30 NONESSENTIAL GRAMMATICAL PRACTICES

假裝你是閉上眼睛、正在好好思考該如何在每一則例句的空格當中，填入最適當的單字和片語，然後就這樣進入夢鄉。睡飽之後把本書悄悄闔上，開始猛K像樣的教材，包準你一定考上！

001

You're (   ). It's written all over your areola.

    (A) laying

    (B) lying

    (C) lied

    (D) nipple

002

(   ) the heat of the moment, I said "I can pitch the turd 100mph."

    (A) Of

    (B) In

    (C) At

    (D) Nipple

003

Though I (   ) killed 9300 people, I was able to make up for it with my inherent perseverance.

    (A) accidented

    (B) accident

    (C) accidentally

    (D) nipply

004

( ) to the state of the ground, the sexual orgy was called off.

(A) On account

(B) Because

(C) Owing

(D) Nipples

005

Stefanie placed her hand on Bob's groin to ( ) his potential.

(A) maximizing

(B) maximized

(C) maximize

(D) nipple?

006

The "Disneyland-Disneysea conflict" turned bloody, ( ) the lives of 7 Mickey Mouses.

(A) costing

(B) coasting

(C) cast

(D) nipple nipple

解答 001～006

001

You're (lying). It's written all over your areola.

(A) laying   (B) lying

(C) lied   (D) nipple

[解答] B

【中譯】你在說謊吧！你的乳暈上都寫得很清楚了。

解說：這是動詞時態的問題。選擇lie「說謊」的現在進行式的(B)lying才對。lie和lay兩個單字經常會出現在考題中，別忘了多念點其它的參考書來熟記它們的正確變化。(D)的「乳頭」不是動詞。

☞ 居然可以寫出謊話，想必這可不是一般的尺寸啊！

002

(In) the heat of the moment, I said "I can pitch the turd 100mph."

(A) Of   (B) In

(C) At   (D) Nipple

[解答] B

【中譯】輸人不輸陣！害我說出「我可以用160公里的時速投出大便」。

解說：這是片語的問題，in the heat of the moment意思是「火氣一來就說大話了。」不只考試會考，在日常生活中也會用到，要好好記熟喔。(D)的「乳頭」不能當前置詞。

☞ 在投到本壘板之前應該就會先在空中四分五裂了。到底是在什麼情況下需要說出這種狠話？

003

Though I (accidentally) killed 9300 people, I was able to make up for it with my inherent perseverance.

(A) accidented   (B) accident

(C) accidentally   (D) nipply

[解答] C

【中譯】雖然我意外地殺了9300人，但靠著我天生的死皮賴臉居然也就大事化小、小事化無了。

解說：這是副詞的問題。從四個答案中選出「意外」的正確副詞變化。對於意外犯錯的人而言是個好用的例句，但是在熟用前還是先改掉自己的毛病比較要緊。(A)的「不平坦的」是形容詞、(B)是名詞，(D)的字尾雖然加了y，但並不會因此就變成副詞。

☞ 看來並不是一般的死皮賴臉。

004

(Owing) to the state of the ground, the sexual orgy was called off.

(A) On account   (B) Because
(C) Owing   (D) Nipples

〔解答〕C

【中譯】因為操場的狀況不好，性派對就取消了。

解說：這是片語的問題。Owing to「因為～的緣故、拜～之賜」。大學入學考中經常出現的問題。(A)On account of～、(B)Because of，兩者的意思都是「因為～的關係」。這三者的其中用法差異已經大幅偏離本書的主旨，在此跳過。(D)是複數，所以並不正確。

☞ 是因為前幾天有下雨嗎？居然要在戶外舉辦……

005

Stefanie placed her hand on Bob's groin to (maximize) his potential.

(A) maximizing   (B) maximized
(C) maximize   (D) nipple?

〔解答〕C

【中譯】史蒂芬妮為了激出鮑伯的最大潛力，將手放在他的胯下。

解說：這是不定詞的問題。因為前面有to，所以選擇動詞的原形。認為不定詞算什麼東西，而堅持要選(A)或(B)的同學很有反骨的精神，不妨這樣保持下去吧！(D)是疑問詞，所以肯定不正確。

☞ 史蒂芬妮到底是何方神聖？究竟可以把什麼發揚光大？

006

The "Disneyland-Disneysea conflict" turned bloody, (costing) the lives of 7 Mickey Mouses.

(A) costing   (B) coasting
(C) cast   (D) nipple nipple

〔解答〕A

【中譯】迪士尼海洋的抗爭演變成流血事件，有7隻米奇因而殉職了。

解說：這是片語的問題。Cost～life是奪走～的性命。因為「奪走」7隻米奇的性命，所以選(A)的costing。turn bloody是「演變成流血事件」，血氣方剛的同學一定要學起來使用。因為前面有to，所以要選擇動詞的原形。認為不定詞算什麼東西，堅持要選發音令人愉快(D)者還是選錯了。

☞ 果然老鼠是生生不息的。啊，不能再說下去了……

007

The (　) said "Kazing", in a roundabout way.

(A) warrior

(B) mage

(C) priest

(D) nipple

008

It's a bird! It's a plane! It's CHAGE (　) ASKA!

(A) and

(B) but

(C) or

(D) nipple

009

Realizing Zhuge Liang (　) his castanet with him, Liu Bei rushed after him.

(A) doesn't take

(B) hadn't taken

(C) hasn't taken

(D) masked nipple

010

Mr. Browne has a large family of 8 (　).

(A) sex dolls

(B) lavatory seats

(C) family chickens

(D) delinquent nipple

011

This is hard to say, but it is impossible to stop (　) a dump at this stage.

(A) dancing

(B) taking

(C) singing

(D) 乳頭

012

Bob's nipples look like (　) in the distance.

(A) Mick Jagger

(B) broccoli

(C) dots

(D) 乳頭

解答 007~012

007

The (priest) said "Kazing", in a roundabout way.

(A) warrior   (B) mage
(C) priest   (D) nipple

[解答]C

【中譯】僧侶不乾不脆地唸了復活咒語「札歐利克」。

解說：這是從句意選出適當單字的問題。所以能不能確實了解kazing「札歐利克」的意思就成了解答的關鍵。札歐利克是在「勇者鬥惡龍」中讓死者復甦的咒語。(A)是「戰士」、(B)是「魔法師」，(D)是「乳頭」，以上名詞均不會唸咒語。因此平常只要有在玩遊戲的人，這一題就可以手到擒來。

☞ 大聲唸出復活咒語，與陰屍路上行走的死人有福同享吧！

008

It's a bird! It's a plane! It's CHAGE (and) ASKA!

(A) and   (B) but
(C) or   (D) nipple

[解答]A

【中譯】是鳥！是飛機！是恰克與飛鳥！

解說：這是接續詞的問題，選出連接恰克與飛鳥的適當接續詞。(B)的「但是」、(C)的「或者」，意思都不通。(D)的乳頭，日本並沒有這個三人團體。

☞ 有沒有其它連接詞比and還適合的呢？

009

Realizing Zhuge Liang (hadn't taken) his castanet with him, Liu Bei rushed after him.

(A) doesn't take   (B) hadn't taken
(C) hasn't taken   (D) masked nipple

[解答]B

【中譯】劉備發現諸葛亮忘記帶響板，急忙追了上去。

解說：這是時態的問題。諸葛亮忘記帶響板是發生在劉備追上去之前就已經完成的事，所以(B)才正確。即使把時態搞錯，不過順著文句的前後意思勉強還是說得過去。(D)即使把乳頭蓋起來也是沒用的。

☞ 軍師作戰還要兼音樂演奏？蜀國的人力不足由此可見一斑。

010

Mr. Browne has a large family of 8 (sex dolls).

(A) sex dolls　　　　(B) lavatory seats
(C) family chickens　(D) delinquent nipple

［解答］A

【中譯】布朗先生擁有8名充氣娃娃的大家庭。

解說：從文意中想像出適當答案的偽文法問題。(B)是「馬桶蓋」，沒常識也要多看電視。(C)的家庭號炸雞並不是你的家人。(A)的充氣娃娃雖然不是生物，但他最接近成為家人的標準。(D)「犯法的乳頭」因為沒有加複數，所以也不正確。

☞ 這樣到底算是幾等親啊？

011

This is hard to say, but it is impossible to stop (taking) a dump at this stage.

(A) dancing　　　　(B) taking
(C) singing　　　　(D) 乳頭

［解答］B

【中譯】雖然很難啟齒，但現階段已經很難阻止大出來了。

解說：這是片語的問題。taking a dump是「排便」的意思。平常在報紙或新聞都看不到這個字，但只要你漸漸熟悉髒話就可迎刃而解了。(D)的乳頭是漢字，所以不正確。選這個的同學傻傻分不清楚英文和漢字，最好休息去看醫生。

☞ 總之先大出來後再傷腦筋處理吧！至於要怎麼處理也沒人知道……

012

Bob's nipples look like (dots) in the distance.

(A) Mick Jagger　　(B) broccoli
(C) dots　　　　　(D) 乳頭

［解答］C

【中譯】鮑伯的乳頭從遠處看像是小點。

解說：這是名詞的問題。「從遠處看」乳頭到底會像什麼？文句的意思讓人浮想聯翩啊！把(A)看成是米克傑格的同學請儘快就醫。(B)的花椰菜不能從遠看，要近看才會像。(D)是中文的「乳頭」，不正確是也。

☞ 真是本世紀的大發現啊！

013

Gundam (   ) the door open for Guntank.

(A) held

(B) have hold

(C) holding

(D) nippless

014

(   ) on to that pubic hair until I get there!

(A) Hangs

(B) Hanging

(C) Hang

(D) I have two nipples.

015

(   ) his father has walking difficulties due to going senile, Bob goes out to buy porn mags for him every day.

(A) As

(B) Because of

(C) Due to

(D) Thousands of nipples.

016

"You'll never know the true (　) of flat chests until you lose them" says Mr. Akamatsu (Age 49, Single)

(A) valuable

(B) valuably

(C) value

(D) Ninip

017

As I'm a virgin, I can't talk about anything (　) technical.

(A) highly

(B) beauty

(C) sexy

(D) nipple

018

I can't see the movie because of the (　) in front of me.

(A) anus

(B) anal

(C) anally

(D) nipple.com

解答 013～018

013

Gundam (held) the door open for Guntank.

   (A) held   (B) have hold

   (C) holding   (D) nippless

［解答］A

【中譯】鋼彈替要通過的鋼坦克檔住門。

解說：這是選出正確動詞時態的問題。(B)要改成has hold才正確。(C)要加上is才是現在進行式，覺得裝模作樣的同學就別學了。(D)的胸貼(蓋住乳頭的OK繃)跟本題無關。

☞ 不愧是一哥，紳士裝甲機器人。

014

(Hang) on to that pubic hair until I get there!

   (A) Hangs   (B) Hanging

   (C) Hang   (D) I have two nipples.

［解答］C

【中譯】在我到達前，抓好陰毛不要放掉！

解說：這是命令句的問題。hang on是抓住～的意思。原形的C是正確答案。選(D)的同學，在此恭喜你了，但並不是正確答案。

☞ 情願抓住稻草也不要抓住陰毛。

015

(As) his father has walking difficulties due to going senile, Bob goes out to buy porn mags for him every day.

   (A) As   (B) Because of

   (C) Due to   (D) Thousands of nipples.

［解答］A

【中譯】鮑伯的父親因為年紀大了行走困難，所以改由他每天去買A書。

解說：這是接續詞的問題。因為後面接的是「複合子句」，所以要選接續詞as。(B)Because of、(C)Due to的後面只能接名詞(句)，所以不正確。希望將來有一天後面可以接「複合子句」。(D)的「幾千個乳頭」，即使數量增加了還是不對。

☞ 英雄難過美人關。鮑伯的父親是英雄還是狗熊就不得而知了。

016

"You'll never know the true (value) of flat chests until you lose them" says Mr. Akamatsu (Age 49, Single)

(A) valuable   (B) valuably
(C) value   (D) Ninip

［解答］C

【中譯】「貧乳的真正價值要等到失去了才會明白。」娓娓道來的赤松氏（49歲、單身）。

解說：這是選擇品詞的問題。在形容詞true的後面要接名詞才對。(A)是形容詞、(B)是副詞，所以都不對。(D)的尼尼普是古代蘇美人主司破壞與殺戮的殘酷夏天太陽神，雖然和乳頭的英文拼法相近，但是意思差了十萬八千里，同學們要注意了。

☞ 不要等到失去了才珍惜。雖然平常也感受不到它們的存在……

017

As I'm a virgin, I can't talk about anything (highly) technical.

(A) highly   (B) beauty
(C) sexy   (D) nipple

［解答］A

【中譯】因為我是處女，所以很抱歉無法回答具有高度專門知識的問題。

解說：這是選擇品詞的問題。首先要分辨technical是形容詞，因此要選可以修飾形容詞的副詞(A)highly。(B)是名詞、(C)是形容詞，所以都不正確。現實生活中要能看出對方是不是童貞，才是勝負的關鍵。(D)回到原點了，還是不正確。

☞ 把你帶回公司讓性愛達人鑑定後再來進行作答。

018

I can't see the movie because of the (anus) in front of me.

(A) anus   (B) anal
(C) anally   (D) nipple.com

［解答］A

【中譯】前面人的肛門擋住害我看不到電影。

解說：這是選擇品詞的問題。接在定冠詞the後面的一定要是名詞。(B)在日語中被當作名詞來使用，其實是形容詞。(C)是副詞，所以名詞anus的(A)才是正確答案。雖然考試不太會出現，但是要好好記住。(D)即使加了網域，也別想矇混過關。

☞ 那倒不如好好欣賞2小時的肛門演出吧？

019

Gundam didn't make the curve and (   ) into the girls' dorm.

(A) stole

(B) smashed

(C) dug

(D) ni, nipple…

020

The new nurse Kristi declares, "I want to make a happy (   )-care unit full of laughter."

(A) incautious

(B) intensive

(C) immodest

(D) intensive nipple

021

Most problems arise from the lack of (   ).

(A) sexy

(B) sexiness

(C) sexed

(D) Oh! These are not my nipples!

022

( ) fact, Uncle Jam has a poor reputation within his neighbourhood.

(A) To

(B) At

(C) In

(D) Ni-pple(1954～2007 France)

023

The heavy rain last week caused ( ) damage to the manager's hair cuticle.

(A) severe

(B) anomalistic

(C) woodtone

(D) nip (　´∀｀)ple

024

Since you are a pervert, I'll ( ) you some slack this time.

(A) cut

(B) get

(C) take

(D) MVN

解答 019～024

019

Gundam didn't make the curve and (smashed) into the girls' dorm.

(A) stole   (B) smashed

(C) dug   (D) ni, nipple…

［解答］B

【中譯】鋼彈轉不過彎，就直接衝進了女生宿合。

解說：這是片語的問題。smash into～是「激烈的衝撞」之意。(A)是潛入，(C)是向下挖，都不符合前半句的文意，所以都不正確；不過(A)的狀況想必是非常開心的。(D)即使語帶哽咽地說，也是不正確的。

☞（尖叫）哇啊，阿姆羅是大色狼！

020

The new nurse Kristi declares, "I want to make a happy (intensive)-care unit full of laughter."

(A) incautious   (B) intensive

(C) immodest   (D) intensive nipple

［解答］B

【中譯】新來的護士克莉絲蒂發下豪語：「我要將加護病房變成充滿歡笑的地方。」

解說：這是省略詞的問題。ICU「加護病房」是intensive-care unit的縮寫。(A)的incautious是「無謀的」，(C)的immodest是「低級的」，(D)的意思是「乳頭加護病房」，但就算集乳起來也沒有意義。

☞ 生病就是氣血有問題，垂危的病人更要集氣才行。

021

Most problems arise from the lack of (sexiness).

(A) sexy   (B) sexiness

(C) sexed   (D) Oh! These are not my nipples!

［解答］B

【中譯】大部分問題的起因都是性感不足所引起的。

解說：這是品詞的問題。of的後面要接名詞，所以選sexiness。(A)是性感的，(C)是性別的、性的，兩者都是形容詞，所以不正確。在此打個岔，要是不知道怎麼稱讚女性時，通常只要說她性感就一定可以搞定。(D)「哇，這不是人家的乳頭！」好像扯太遠了，事實上真的瞎～很～大～！

☞ 性感不足固然危險，但過度攝取性感同樣危險。過與不及都足以致命。

022

(In) fact, Uncle Jam has a poor reputation within his neighbourhood.

(A) To   (B) At
(C) In   (D) Ni-pple(1954～2007 France)

［解答］C

【中譯】事實上，果醬爺爺的鄰居都給他負評。

解說：這是前置詞的問題。In fact是「事實上」的意思，這是大學考試必有的基礎片語，即使不想記也會不知不覺就記住的最好範例，所以同學們不用在這裡死背了。(D)的「你破崙」取得好像歷史人物名字是不正確的。

☞ 問題大概來自於他亂丟烤失敗麵包超人的臉，讓人看了都害怕。

023

The heavy rain last week caused (severe) damage to the manager's hair cuticle.

(A) severe   (B) anomalistic
(C) woodtone   (D) nip（ ´∀`）ple

［解答］A

【中譯】上禮拜的大雨造成經理毛鱗片嚴重的損傷。

解說：這是形容詞的問題。可以修飾damage的適當形容詞是(A)「嚴重的」。(B)是「異常的」。(C)是「木紋的」，雖然意思不通，但是手拿武器據理力爭，說不定就能講通。(D)即使挾帶表情符號還是不正確。

☞ 經理表皮之外的損害更令人在乎吧！

024

Since you are a pervert, I'll (cut) you some slack this time.

(A) cut   (B) get
(C) take   (D) MVN

［解答］A

【中譯】看在你是變態的份上，這次就睜一隻眼閉一隻眼吧！

解說：這是片語的問題。cut (someone) some slack是「對(某人)睜一隻眼閉一隻眼」的意思。選擇(B)(C)的答案也無法視而不見，只能說抱歉了。(D)MVN是「Most Valuable Nipple最有價值乳頭」的縮寫，雖然很想看，但還是不正確。

☞ 天下無難事，只怕有變態。

025

On December 8th, Gunma Prefecture ( ) launched its fifth man-powered spacecraft "Yagibushi 5."

(A) successfully

(B) success

(C) successful

(D) sonic nipple

026

( ) your pride and accept the diaper.

(A) Swallow

(B) Eat

(C) Throw

(D) A helping of nipple

027

If my neighbour's pubic hair intrudes on my property, am I within my rights to trim ( )?

(A) it

(B) them

(C) themselves

(D) The Return of nipple

028

The purpose of this pubic hair is to replace confidence (　) doubt.

(A) to

(B) in

(C) with

(D) ＊ ＊

029

Throw down your (　) sweet potato and come out with your hands up!

(A) baked

(B) baking

(C) bakes

(D) My name is Nipple.

030

The right and left (　) have different functions.

(A) chin

(B) bellybutton

(C) anus

(D) nipple

解答 025～030

025

On December 8th,Gunma Prefecture (successfully) launched its fifth man-powered spacecraft "Yagibushi 5."

    (A) successfully   (B) success   (C) successful   (D) sonic nipple

﹝解答﹞A

【中譯】12月8日群馬縣成功發射了第5艘人力的太空船「八木節5號」。

解說：這是品詞的問題。可以修飾動詞launched的只有(A)的副詞successfully。Success是各種考試經常出現的單字，將它的動詞、名詞、形容詞、副詞的各種變化記熟，同學們也就可以出人頭地了。(D)的「音速乳頭」不明其義，完全不正確。

☞ 就不能替太空船取個很威的名字嗎？

026

(Swallow) your pride and accept the diaper.

    (A) Swallow   (B) Eat   (C) Throw   (D) A helping of nipple

﹝解答﹞A

【中譯】把自尊拋棄吧，這是你的尿布！

解說：這是片語的問題。swallow one's pride是拋棄～的自尊，雖然這裡用拋棄，在英語中卻是用swallow吞下去、嚥回去來表現。這大概也是東西方價值觀不同之處吧。順帶一提，在中國是講油煎自尊、在韓國是講把自尊泡在泡菜裡。(D)的意思是「大份乳頭」，不論東西方都是錯的答案。

☞ 自尊怎麼拋棄？是想吐出來才對吧！

027

If my neighbour's pubic hair intrudes on my property, am I within my rights to trim (it)?

    (A) it   (B) them
    (C) themselves   (D) The Return of nipple

﹝解答﹞A

【中譯】如果隔壁家的陰毛伸到我家的院子來，可以剪掉它嗎？

解說：這是代名詞的問題。Hair是不可計算的名詞，所以視為單數。就算不知道，只要注意到intrude加上了第三人稱單數的s，應該就會選正確答案的(A)。pubic的拼法很像public，就算注意到了也不會加分。(D)的「回來了，乳頭」雖然令人很好奇之前跑去了哪裡，但還是不正確。

☞ 民法中規定鄰居家的樹枝即使伸過來也不能隨意修剪，更何況是陰毛！

028

The purpose of this pubic hair is to replace confidence (with) doubt.

(A) to　　　　　　　(B) in
(C) with　　　　　　(D) ＊＊

［解答］C

【中譯】這根陰毛的企圖是把人們的信賴變成懷疑。

解說：這是前置詞的問題。replace A with B是把A變成B的意思。注意不要憑感覺選到(A)的to。(D)大概是想以「＊」來代表乳頭，但依然是錯的。

☞ 毛雖小志不小，令人誠惶誠恐。

029

Throw down your (baked) sweet potato and come out with your hands up!

(A) baked　　　　　(B) baking
(C) bakes　　　　　(D) My name is Nipple.

［解答］A

【中譯】丟下你的烤地瓜，雙手舉起站出來！

解說：這是分詞的問題。地瓜是「被烤的」，所以選(A)baked。注意不要選成了baking「烤」。(D)初次見面，你是錯的。

☞ 本來想用烤地瓜來抵抗嗎？

030

The right and left (nipple) have different functions.

(A) chin　　　　　　(B) bellybutton
(C) anus　　　　　　(D) nipple

［解答］D

【中譯】右乳頭和左乳頭的功能不一樣。

解說：這是常識的問題。左右兩邊都有的不是(A)下巴、(B)肚臍和(C)肛門，而是(D)的乳頭。辛苦了，終於輪到你是對的了！

☞ 同功不同頭。

索引
INDEX

English
全民英檢篇

續·偽英語教科書

作　　者／中山
插　　畫／千野A
譯　　者／錢亞東

發 行 人／黃鎮隆
協　　理／陳君平
資深主編／袁珮玲
美術總監／沙雲佩
封面設計／陳碧雲
公關宣傳／邱小祐、陶若瑤

出　　版／城邦文化事業股份有限公司　尖端出版
　　　　　台北市民生東路二段141號10樓
　　　　　電話：(02)2500-7600　傳真：(02)2500-1975
　　　　　讀者服務信箱：spp_books@mail2.spp.com.tw
發　　行／英屬蓋曼群島商家庭傳媒股份有限公司
　　　　　城邦分公司　尖端出版
　　　　　台北市民生東路二段141號10樓
　　　　　電話：(02)2500-7600(代表號)　傳真：(02)2500-1979
　　　　　劃撥專線／(03)312-4212
　　　　　劃撥戶名：英屬蓋曼群島商家庭傳媒(股)公司城邦分公司
　　　　　劃撥帳號：50003021
　　　　　※劃撥金額未滿500元，請加付掛號郵資50元
法律顧問／通律機構　台北市重慶南路二段59號11樓

台灣地區總經銷／中彰投以北(含宜花東)　高見文化行銷股份有限公司
　　　　　　　　電話：0800-055-365　傳真：(02)2668-6220
　　　　　　　　雲嘉以南　威信圖書有限公司
　　　　　　　　(嘉義公司)電話：0800-028-028　傳真：(05)233-3863
　　　　　　　　(高雄公司)電話：0800-028-028　傳真：(07)373-0087
馬新地區總經銷／城邦(馬新)出版集團　Cite(M) Sdn.Bhd.(458372U)
　　　　　　　　電話：(603)9057-8822、9056-3833　傳真：(603)9057-6622
　　　　　　　　E-mail：cite@cite.com.my
　　　　　　　　大眾書局(新加坡)　POPULAR(Singapore)
　　　　　　　　電話：65-6462-9555　傳真：65-6468-3710
　　　　　　　　E-mail：feedback@popularworld.com
　　　　　　　　大眾書局(馬來西亞)　POPULAR(Malaysia)
　　　　　　　　電話：603-9179-6333　傳真：03-9179-6200、03-9179-6339
　　　　　　　　客服諮詢熱線：1-300-88-6336
　　　　　　　　E-mail：popularmalaysia@popularworld.com

版　　次／2014年12月初版　Printed in Taiwan　ISBN 978-957-10-5735-4

國家圖書館出版品預行編目資料

續·偽英語教科書 [全民英檢篇]／中山 著 --
初版 --臺北市：尖端, 2014.12
　　面；公分
　　ISBN 978-957-10-5735-4(平裝)

1. 英語　2. 詞彙

805.12　　　　　　　　　　103016723